BOITANO'S EDGE

BOITANO'S EDGE

Inside the Real World of Figure Skating

WRITTEN BY

BRIAN BOITANO

WITH SUZANNE HARPER

INTRODUCTION BY

PEGGY FLEMING

SIMON & SCHUSTER

For my parents, who have always supported me, with love
—B. B.

For my parents, with love
—S. H.

SIMON & SCHUSTER
1230 Avenue of the Americas
New York, New York 10020

Text copyright © 1997 by Brian Boitano with Suzanne Harper.
Pages 142-143 constitute an extension of the copyright page.

Book design by Christy Hale
The text for this book is set in 14.5 point Centaur.
Printed and bound in the United States of America
First Edition
10 9 8 7 6 5 4 3 2 1

Library of Congress Cataloging-in-Publication Data
Boitano, Brian.
Boitano's edge: inside the real world of figure skating / written by Brian Boitano
with Suzanne Harper.
p. cm.
Summary: Olympic ice skating champion Brian Boitano describes the sport of
figure skating and his own experiences as a skater.
ISBN 0-689-81915-3
1. Skating—Juvenile literature. 2. Boitano, Brian—Juvenile literature.
3. Skaters—United States—Biography—Juvenile literature.
4. Skating—Records—Juvenile literature.
[1. Boitano, Brian. 2. Ice skaters. 3. Ice skating.]
I. Harper, Suzanne. II. Title.
GV849.B64 1998
746.91'2'092—dc21
[B] 97-29498

TABLE OF CONTENTS

I'VE ALWAYS SAID THAT FIGURE SKATING IS THE most revealing sport of all.

Not only are we usually all alone out on that ice, but we're being judged for so many very personal things: our costume, the music we chose, and how we move to that music. It's very hard to hide what kind of person you really are with so many aspects of your personality being watched.

Now Brian Boitano has written a book that takes you behind the scenes of the sport of figure skating and does it in a fun format. He's the perfect choice to write a book like this because Brian knows skating from every side. He remembers what it's like to be nervous about your very first lesson, and he also knows what it feels like to win an Olympic gold medal. He knows what it's like to skate in an ice show, and what it's like to create and produce his own ice show. And Brian knows that this is a sport that can be enjoyed on many, many different levels.

When Brian won in Calgary in 1988, he set the standard for our sport, and he has never let it slip. For some skaters, that gold medal would have been the pinnacle, but Brian has influenced the sport of figure skating even more as a professional. The "Boitano Rule" shoved open the door of Olympic competition for professional skaters, and began a new era when amateurs were finally allowed to earn money for their skating without losing their Olympic eligibility.

Nine years after Brian himself turned professional, he has refused to compromise any aspect of his skating. Even today, his athleticism, technical level and performance qualities are unmatched...but it is his inner strength, focus, and dedication that make him such a great role model. Those values, combined with talent and a solid work ethic, are why Brian continues to push figure skating to its limits.

And why he will never settle for less.

—Peggy Fleming
1968 Olympic Gold Medalist

$\mathcal{I}$ LOVE SKATING. I LOVE THE SPEED, the power, the excitement, the feeling that—even for just a moment—I can defy gravity and fly through the air. And I love the way that a great skating performance, like any work of art, can move an audience to laughter or tears.

I've devoted most of my life to skating. As a kid, I spent hours at the rink, learning to jump and spin—and dreaming about winning an Olympic gold medal.

After years of training, my dream came true at the 1988 Winter Olympics. In the years since then, I've seen the popularity of skating soar. Almost 100,000 kids belong to the United States Figure Skating Association; many more take lessons and skate at their local rinks. More competitions, both amateur and professional, are held every year; many of them win huge ratings on television. In fact, a recent survey reveals that figure skating is the second most popular sport (behind only NFL football) in the United States.

Perhaps that's no surprise. When a skater steps on the ice to compete, the nerves, tension, and sheer *suspense* of that moment make for great drama.

But the actual competition reflects only a small part of what figure skating is all about. There are other aspects to skating, hidden to everyone except other skaters. I'd like to take you inside that world—the one that's been my home for twenty-five years—and show you what it's like to train as a skater, to challenge yourself to be the best, to push the sport in new directions.

This is the *real* figure skating world, and it's the part I love the most: when it's just me, an empty rink, and the ice.

Brian Boitano

Dave Black

THE EVENT: The 1988 Olympic Winter Games
THE PLACE: Calgary, Alberta, Canada
THE DATE: February 20, 1988

FTER SIXTEEN YEARS OF HARD work and training, sixteen years of practicing in cold rinks at dawn, sixteen years of jumping into the air, crashing to the ice, and getting up to do it all over again, I was standing on Olympic ice.

My lifelong dream was about to come true—or about to be dashed. I would know in four and a half minutes.

The long program was the last part of the competition. I was ahead of the Canadian skater Brian Orser in the compulsory figures, which counted for thirty percent of the score; he was ahead of me in the short program, which counted for twenty percent. This placed me first by a small margin. On that night, we were in a dead heat for the Olympic gold medal. Now we were set to skate the long program, and the final showdown—what the press had dubbed the "Battle of the Brians"—was about to take place.

By the luck of the draw, I was skating first in the final group. That was my favorite position, even though it was harder to score high marks; I liked to set the standard. But on this night, I knew that I had to skate the best performance of my life.

My choreographer, Sandra Bezic, had created majestic and emotional programs for both my short and long programs. Before I stepped on the ice, she said, "It's your moment. Show them your soul."

I paused and looked into the eyes of my coach, Linda

At the 1988 U.S. National Championships, I celebrated the composition and style marks for my short program (opposite page) with my coach Linda Leaver and my choreographer Sandra Bezic (below). I received eight 6.0s and one 5.9. That was the first time I received a 6.0, the highest mark possible. Months later, I skated the same program at the 1988 Winter Olympics.

Leaver. We had worked together for this moment since I was eight years old. As usual, we didn't need to speak. She said what needed to be said—*You can do it*—with her eyes. I nodded, took a deep breath, and took to the ice.

As I circled the ice, waiting for the announcer to call my name, I heard my brother yell from the stands, "Boitano!" Someone in another part of the audience yelled, "Orser!"

It turned into a call-and-response chant: "Boitano!" "Orser!" "Boitano!" "Orser!"

At the same time, two voices were echoing in my head. One voice kept saying, "You're going to blow it!" But the other one was saying, "You *won't* blow it. That's not who you are. You know how to do this."

As I kept on circling, I did what I always do at that moment in a competition: I asked for help from the universe. I thought, "Please help me, because I can't do this by myself."

Then the announcer's voice boomed over the speakers: "Representing the United States of America, Brian Boitano!"

As I skated to center ice, the audience chant died out, but I was no longer aware of the crowd. I was totally centered in the moment; all my attention was focused on skating well.

Music from the film soundtrack *Napoleon* filled the arena. For eleven seconds, I held my opening position and counted my breaths; I knew exactly how many I needed to take before making my first move.

After years of work, I waited to begin my long program at the 1988 Winter Olympics.

Four, five, six… This was it. I turned my head and pushed off, talking myself through each move in my mind. *Stretch and turn, one, two, three, mohawk, back, drop, back, arm…*

As I started my program, I looked down the ice and imagined that the rink was separated into sections by a dozen golden fences. I used that imagery to remind myself to take one thing at a time; I told myself to wait until I passed each fence before thinking of the next jump or spin I had to complete.

I launched my first jump, the 'Tano triple Lutz with my arm overhead. Up … down … perfect! Then a triple Axel-double toe loop combination, a triple flip, a flying camel spin, a triple Salchow, a death drop, all connected by footwork. Next my most difficult move, a triple flip-triple toe loop combination that seemed so easy tonight it felt as if angels were lifting me and spinning me. Now a spread eagle that lasted almost fifteen seconds, and a chance to breathe.

Everything was going perfectly, just as I had dreamed for so many years. I passed center ice and the red hockey circle that served as my landmark. I was right on track for my last jump, another triple Axel.

All I needed was one last burst of energy, one last launch into the air. Usually, I'm thinking technically as I approach a jump: how much speed I need, what angle my body should be at, and so on. But for that jump, every technical thought went out of my head. All I kept thinking was, "Please, please, please . . . "

I jumped. Rotated three and a half times in the air. Landed on one-quarter of an inch of tempered steel. The blade gripped the ice. It held.

That was the turning point of my program, because I knew I needed two triple Axels to win. I smiled and let myself have five seconds to enjoy landing the Axel, then it was back to business. If I didn't stay focused, I could make a mistake on a much easier move and possibly lose my chance at the gold medal.

As I finished my program, I threw my head back and said "thank you" for the performance of my life. I felt so happy and so proud that I was laughing and crying at the same time. "Yes!" I thought. "I did it!"

Now came the really hard part.

Waiting.

First American figure skater to win an Olympic gold medal: Dick Button in 1948. He was eighteen years old.

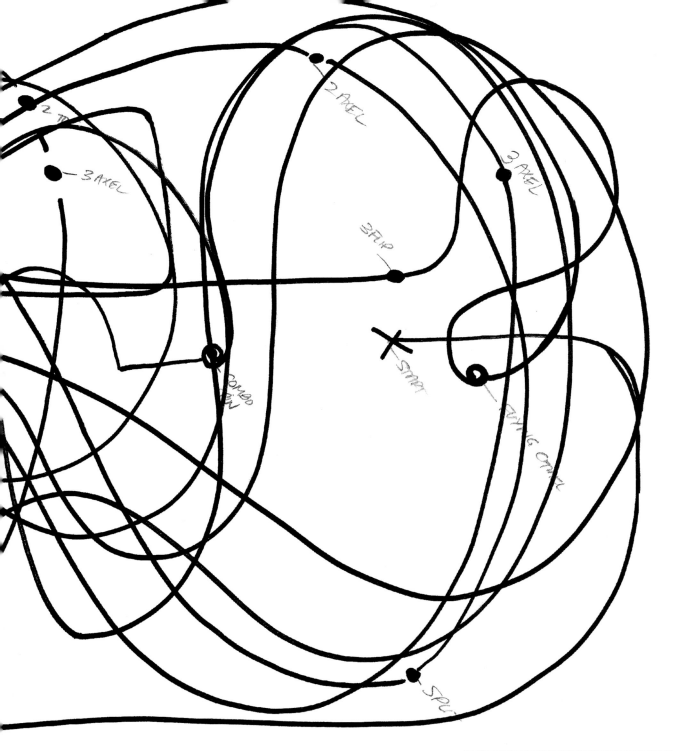

2 T

3 AXEL

2 AXEL

3 AXEL

3 FLIP

COMBO
...

X—START

FLYING CAMEL

SPI...

I drew this blueprint of my 1988 Olympic long program from memory; I don't think I'll ever forget it. I did a spiral toward the beginning of the program (far left); a spread eagle in the middle (left); and an arabian at the end (right).

The judges awarded my program excellent marks, all 5.8s and 5.9s. In a way, my scores didn't even matter. I was so happy with the way I had skated that the marks were almost incidental.

I knew that Brian Orser was about to take the ice after me. I went to the dressing room, changed, and grabbed my Walkman. Sitting in the bathroom, I listened to music over the headphones for the length of time that I knew it would take for Orser to step onto the ice, skate his program, and be awarded his marks.

After five minutes, I pulled off my headphones, just in time to hear the announcer boom out Orser's final mark: 6.0, which is the highest mark possible.

That was it. I had lost. I knew it. His scores were too good.

I walked over to the mirror and stared at my reflection. "That's okay," I thought. "I skated great. That's what counts. I can keep competing and aim for the next Olympics in four more years. That's okay."

Then my teammate Christopher Bowman entered the dressing room. He had a strange smile on his face. He held up one finger. Number one.

Chris's fondness for pranks was well-known in the skating community.

"If this is a practical joke," I told him, "I'm going to kill you."

"No," Chris said. "You won. You really won."

"That can't be true. I heard his last mark. He got a 6.0."

But that 6.0, Chris told me, was the only perfect mark Brian Orser had received. He had stepped out of his triple flip. He had doubled his last Axel. He had skated wonderfully, but those mistakes had cost him.

I still had to wait for Viktor Petrenko of the Soviet Union to skate. The way the scores stood, if one judge placed him first and knocked me to second, Brian Orser could win. Chris sat with me as I nervously paced the floor. Then the team doctor burst into the dressing room to tell me the news.

"You won! You won the gold medal!"

(Opposite page) I was floating on a cloud right after the Olympic medal ceremony. When I look at this picture, I think, "I can't believe that was me!"

I perform the 'Tano Triple—a triple Lutz with one arm overhead—in my long program (left).

This is my Olympic gold medal, shown actual size (right).

WINTER OLYMPIC GOLD MEDALS

Is the gold medal really gold? Not totally. Both gold and silver medals are made of 92.5 percent pure silver. The gold medal is then plated with at least six grams of gold. The design on a gold medal varies from one Winter Olympics to the next. The organizing committee of each host city decides how the medal will look. No matter what design is chosen, most of the gold medals are about 60 millimeters in diameter and three millimeters thick.

(Breaking with tradition, the 1992 Winter Olympic Games medals in Albertville, France, were made of Lalique glass encased in gold, silver, or bronze metal frames; and the medals for the 1994 Games in Lillehammer, Norway, were made from green granite stone.)

GLOSSARY

Amateur: A skater who is allowed to compete in events sanctioned by the United States Figure Skating Association and the International Skating Union, such as the U.S. National Championships, the World Championships, and the Olympic Games. See also *eligible*.

Artistic merit: The judge's mark awarded for the skater's overall presentation, including creative choreography, innovative moves, musicality, and beautiful execution of moves.

Blade: The metal part of an ice skate that comes into contact with the ice.

Boot: The shoelike part of an ice skate which covers a skater's foot.

Bracket: A turn that's made on one foot, moving from forward to backward or backward to forward; during the turn, the skater changes edges counter to the circle rotation.

Character: A part or role representing a person; for example, an actor who plays a part is said to be playing a character.

Choctaw: A turn from a forward inside edge to a backward outside edge that requires a change of foot.

Choreography: The art of composing the movements, steps, and patterns of a dance.

Combination: Two or more jumps done in a row, with no steps in between, or two or more spins done consecutively without stopping.

Competitive program: The program a skater uses during a competition (as opposed to an exhibition program, which is usually less difficult and performed during a show or other non-judged event).

Competitive season: The months in which competitions are held; for example, a competitive season could start in November and last until March.

Compulsory dance: A set-pattern dance with specified steps, timing, rhythm, partner positions, and musical mood.

Counter: A turn that is a bracket turn going in and a three-turn coming out with the skater remaining on the same edge throughout.

Crossovers: The stroking a skater uses when moving forward or backward; the foot that crosses over is set on the inside edge and the foot that is being crossed over is on the outside edge.

Dance: A skating discipline in which a man and a woman focus on intricate footwork and body movements to express the rhythm and mood of different types of music. No throws are allowed, and jumps and spins are limited.

Double: Any jump that consists of two (or, in the case of the Axel, two and a half) revolutions in the air.

Edges: The two sharp sides of the skate blade on either side of the grooved center.

Edge jump: A jump in which the skater takes off from the edge of one blade.

Eligible: A skater who is allowed to compete in events sanctioned by the United States Figure Skating Association and the International Skating Union, such as the U.S. National Championships, the World Championships, and the Olympic Games. See also *amateur*.

Figures: The figure eight and variations of the figure eight which skaters used to perform in competition as part of the compulsory phase. Also called "compulsory figures" or "school figures."

Flying: Extending and moving swiftly through the air.

Footwork: A sequence of steps, turns, hops, and changes of positions.

Free dance: A part of an ice dancing competition in which the couple skates for a certain length of time to music and choreography of their own choice.

Free foot, hip, knee, side, etc.: The foot a skater is not skating on at any one time is the free foot; everything on that side of the body is called "free."

Freestyle: A part of a singles competition in which the skater performs jumps, spins and footwork to music. The short program, long program, and exhibitions are freestyle skating.

Gold medalist: A skater who has passed all the tests in a particular discipline of skating. (Note: This term does not refer to a skater who has won a gold medal in competition.)

Hockey stop: A method of stopping very fast on the ice; the skater throws both heels out to the right and makes a sharp, quick turn perpendicular to the line of travel and stops.

Hollow: The groove that runs the length of the skate blade and creates the edges.

Hop: A move that consists of a lift off the ice with no revolution in the air.

Jump: A move that consists of a lift off the ice with revolution in the air.

Landing: The part of the jump or hop when the skater touches the ice after being in the air.

Lean: The body's position when it forms an angle less than 90 degrees relative to the ice.

Lift: A move in which the male skater raises his female partner over his head.

Long program: The freestyle program in the singles and pair events; it lasts four to four and a half minutes, with no set elements.

Marks: The scores given to a skater by the judges.

Mohawk: A turn from front to back that involves a change of foot with no change of edge.

Motion memory: The feel or sense within a skater's body of how to correctly perform a move.

Non-eligible: A skater who is not allowed to compete in events sanctioned by the United States Figure Skating Association and the International Skating Union, such as the U.S. National Championships, the World Championships, and the Olympic Games. See also *professional*.

One-foot jump: A jump in which the takeoff foot and landing foot are the same and the landing is on a back inside edge.

Ordinal: The ranking that a judge gives a skater (for example, if a judge ranks a skater first, that skater has received a first-place ordinal).

Original set-pattern dance: A set-pattern dance with a prescribed rhythm created by the ice dancing couple.

Patch: Time on the ice used for practicing figures. The term comes from the fact that each skater has his own "patch" of ice on which to practice.

Pattern: The path followed by a skater as seen by the resulting tracings on the ice.

Pivot: A two-foot spin with one toe in the ice.

Professional: A skater who is not allowed to compete in events sanctioned by the United States Figure Skating Association and the International Skating Union, such as the U.S. National Championships, the World Championships, and the Olympic Games. See also *non-eligible*.

Proficiency tests: A series of United States Figure Skating Association (USFSA) tests to measure a skater's progress and determine which competitive level he has achieved.

Quad: A four-revolution jump.

Radius: The skate blade's curvature as seen from the side.

Regional: A competitive division, based on a certain area of the country; skaters who win at this level advance to the Sectionals.

Required element: A skating move, such as a particlular jump or spin, that must be done in a short program.

Revolution: Turning, particularly in the air.

Rocker: A turn from forward to backward with the first part consisting of a three-turn and the second part of a bracket.

Roll: A deep outside edge.

Rotation: The process of turning.

Scissors: Quick movement of the free foot forward and backward while executing a turn in a figure.

Sculling: Movements of the skater's feet swaying in and out in order to move across the ice.

Sectional: A competitive division, based on a certain area of the country, that leads to the U.S. National Championship; skaters who win at this level advance to Nationals.

Sequence: A continuous or connected series.

Serpentine: Footwork that curves back and forth across the rink.

Short program: A two-minute freestyle program for single and pair skaters that contains seven required elements.

Single: A one-revolution (or, in the case of an Axel, a one-and-a-half revolution) jump.

Skate guards: The plastic protectors that are put on skate blades to protect them when skaters walk off the ice. Also called "guards."

Skating foot, hip, knee, side, etc.: The foot the skater is skating on at any one time is the skating foot; everything on that side of the body is then called "skating."

Snowplow: A beginner's method of stopping on ice by angling the heel of one foot and skidding across the blade's inside edge with both skates on the ice.

Spin: A move in which the skater turns rapidly in one spot on the ice.

Strike-off: The initial push-off from a stationary position.

Stroking: The basic skating movement in which the skater pushes off by pressing the entire blade of the free foot into the ice and thrusting the free leg back and away from the body while bending the skating knee.

T-stop: A method of stopping on the ice in which the skater puts his blades in a T position, and skids to a stop along the blades' outside edge.

Takeoff: The lift-off edge on a jump.

Technical merit: The judge's mark awarded for the skater's athletic achievement, including the difficulty of moves.

Telegraph: To indicate to the audience that a certain move, especially a jump, is coming up; not considered good skating style: "He still telegraphs his jumps too much."

Tempo: The speed at which music is played.

Three-turn: A turn from forward to backward in which there is a change of edge; the turn rotates with the circle being skated and leaves a tracing that looks like a 3.

Throw: A pairs move in which the male partner lifts his partner and propels her into the air.

Thrust: A pushing motion that propels the skater across the ice.

Title: A championship; for example, if a skater wins the gold medal at the World Championships, he's said to have won the world title.

Toe-assisted jumps: Jumps in which the free toe is placed in the ice to assist lift-off; the leg acts as a pole vault.

Toe picks: The teeth or points on the front of a skate blade.

Tour: A journey of a skating show from town to town for a series of performances.

Tracings: The marks left on the ice by the skate.

Triple: A three-revolution (or, in the case of the Axel, a three-and-a-half revolution) jump.

Waltz jump: A beginner's jump that involves half a revolution in the air, taken from a forward outside edge and landed on the other foot's back outside edge.

Zamboni: The machine that shaves the ice and spreads fresh water to provide a clean surface.

Dave Black

WHEN I WAS EIGHT YEARS OLD, I
was a daredevil roller skater on the sidewalks of Sunnyvale,
California, where I grew up. I spent every waking moment
on my roller skates.

Then my mom took me to see an ice show and I was
hooked. I had never seen anything like that before; it
was athletic and challenging and exciting and fast. Skating
was just really cool. So after that, when I roller-skated, I'd
pretend that our driveway was an ice surface. I'd draw
chalk marks that were supposed to be the lines made by
a blade on the ice. I'd put a blanket around my neck and
pretend that it was a cape and that I was Rudolph
Valentino, starring with Peggy Fleming. I'd even make little billboards out of wood, announcing the show I was
starring in: PEGGY FLEMING, STARRING WITH RUDOLPH
VALENTINO.

I have no idea why I decided to take the name Rudolph
Valentino! He was a silent film star known for his mys-
terious presence and good looks; maybe that's what I
thought I wanted to be when I was an adult—or maybe
it was just the most famous name I knew. Of course,
Rudolph Valentino never put on a pair of skates, but that
didn't matter to me.

When my roller skates got too small, I'd cut out the
toes so that I could keep wearing them for months and
months. My toes stuck out of the ends of the boots, but
I kept skating. My mom remembers that when I wore
hand-me-down skates that were too large, I'd put on
sneakers and *then* put on my skates over them. Once my
kindergarten teacher passed by our house and saw me
doing all these jumps and spins on my roller skates. She

SKATING PARENTS

My parents were great because they let me be an individual and have my own life. They dropped me off at the rink and left. When I got home, they'd ask me how my day went and I'd tell them, then we'd talk about other things. A lot of parents ask their kids, "How many triples did you land today?" They pressure them too much. Skating can build a kid's self-esteem, but not if he's expected to win a certain championship. There are too many factors involved in winning to put that kind of expectation on a kid.

My parents were supportive—they made sure I got to practice and they bought my lessons and ice time—but they knew that skating was my sport, not theirs. They've never taken any credit for my skating, but they're one of the major reasons for my success.

just stopped and stared. Then she asked my mom where I learned to skate like that. My mom told her that I had taught myself. I was kind of an unusual sight in my neighborhood, I guess.

We had a kidney bean-shaped patio in the back of the house that I also pretended was an ice rink. I'd turn on the record player in the living room and open the patio doors and skate to the music. I remember loving "Gypsy Woman" and Carly Simon's song, "That's the Way I Always Heard It Should Be."

Even as I was pretending to skate on ice, I was begging to try ice skating for real. At the time, I was on a baseball team and my dad was the coach, but I just kept saying, "I want to go ice skating. I want to go ice skating."

My parents finally took me to an ice rink in Sunnyvale that was four minutes away from our house. We got out of the car and went inside the building—and then the strangest thing happened. I suddenly remembered that I had been there before with my two older sisters and brother when I was about four years old.

When I walked into the rink for the second time, that memory came flooding back and I had the same feeling that I'd had when I was four: total awe. There was a fireplace in the lobby. The walls in the rink were painted a beautiful blue and the ice was a brilliant white. People were skating around this huge, grand space. It was like no place I'd ever seen; as a kid, it seemed almost otherworldly.

That's when I gave up baseball. Not only was I crazy about skating, but *everybody* played baseball and I didn't

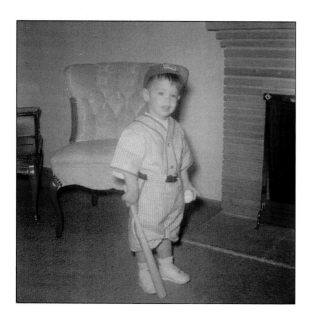

want to be like everybody else. I also liked playing a solo sport, rather than a team sport. I actually *liked* the feeling that if I made a mistake, I couldn't blame anybody but myself. A lot of skaters get into the habit of blaming their coaches for mistakes that they make; they even switch coaches because of that. But, to me, the whole point of skating—the freedom of it—depends on being self-reliant.

The rink offered six levels of group lessons for kids who wanted to learn to skate. After finishing those group lessons, kids who wanted more instruction took

(Left) Baseball didn't have much of a chance once I discovered skating.

(Opposite page) I was ten years old in the top two photos and eight in the bottom one. I was really trying hard to touch my toes in the split jump—although I couldn't quite make it back then.

LEARNING THE BASICS

The United States Figure Skating Association (USFSA) has developed a standard core curriculum to be used in group lessons. As its name indicates, the "Basic Skills" program teaches skaters the fundamentals of the sport.

The program is divided into the following tracks: Snowplow Sam, for very young skaters; Basic Skills; Freestyle; Figure; Dance; Team, which teaches the basics of precision skating; Power Freestyle; Hockey; and Power Hockey.

Many clubs and rinks teach the programs through weekly group classes. Each track consists of four to six levels. For example, the Basic Skills track includes six levels. At Basic 1, skaters learn such moves as sitting on the ice and getting up from a kneeling position, skating across the rink without falling, and doing a snowplow stop. By Basic 6, the skater progresses to mohawks, three turns, and forward crossovers.

The USFSA also conducts a series of proficiency tests for skaters which become progressively more difficult. At all USFSA sanctioned competitions, skaters are grouped with others who have passed the same level of tests.

Test sessions are held by most skating clubs affiliated with the USFSA. Skaters join a USFSA club when they're competing on an amateur level. Beginning skaters get experience being judged at small, inter-club competitions. As a skater passes more tests, he's eligible to enter Regional competitions, which are the first step on the road to the U.S. National Championships and, ultimately, the World Championships and Olympics.

Terry Kubicka

MY SKATING HERO

My idol was Terry Kubicka, the 1975 U.S. National Champion. He was ahead of his time; he did every triple, consistently, and was a great technical skater. He did a back flip in the 1976 Olympics, a move that was later outlawed in amateur competition.

I saw him skate in person in 1972, when he and Dorothy Hamill guest starred in a show put on by the Silver Edge Figure Skating Club in Sunnyvale, which later turned into the Peninsula Figure Skating Club. The show was called "We're On Our Way." It was one of my first ice shows. I played Ernie the Muppet, and did my first spread eagle in a performance.

The World Figure Skating Museum

private lessons. After I went skating a couple more times, I started group lessons and went every Saturday for a month. Each week, I advanced to the next level.

The fifth week, I went to the rink and I met a skating teacher named Linda Leaver. To pass that week's class, I had to learn a two-foot spin. I was trying so hard to go fast that I kept falling down.

I remember Linda saying, "Brian, all you have to do is stay upright and you'll pass this class. Don't try so hard." But I wanted to spin incredibly fast, so I kept falling. Finally, she got me to calm down enough to stay up and finish the spin, and I passed the class.

After my last class, Linda talked to my parents. She told them that she thought I was ready for private lessons and that she'd like to teach me.

My parents went to the rink with me and discussed schedules, ice costs, and lessons with Linda. Linda politely suggested that my Sears skates would have to go. From that time on, I wore Harlick boots with Wilson blades. I vividly remember my first private lesson. I remember that Linda was wearing a yellow one-piece ski suit. I remember that the rink was really crowded. And I remember the magical feeling when the rink lights changed colors.

When I started taking private lessons, my mom tells me that I only skated a couple of times a week at first. In my memory, though, my entire life revolved around wanting to go to the ice rink. If I wasn't skating, I was thinking about skating; I was always at the rink in my mind or I was on my roller skates in the driveway. So I feel that I skated every day as a kid.

I wasn't the most talented skater on the ice. But I was athletic—all that roller-skating had probably helped my coordination—and I was a really hard worker. I stayed on the ice until they kicked me off. I loved getting better and better every day.

I learned almost all the single revolution jumps in that first private lesson. It wasn't hard at all; in fact, it was fun. I never thought that I couldn't do it. I believe that it's written somewhere what you're supposed to do with your life. I was only eight years old, but I felt that I had found what I was destined to do: skate.

I always loved the camaraderie of skating in ice shows. I was nine when I skated in my first show (I'm on the far left).

HOW FIGURE SKATING GOT ITS NAME

(Top)
Figure skating got its name from the elaborate figures that skaters would etch on the ice.

(Middle)
During a figures competition, skaters and coaches watch competitors from the rail, but it's hard to tell how good the figures are from that vantage point. So after the competition, a lot of people go onto the ice to see the figures up close.

(Bottom)
Janet Lynn was one of the best freestyle skaters ever.

Figure skating gets its name from "figures," the art of tracing variations on the figure eight on the ice. In the late eighteenth and early nineteenth centuries, the English took this aspect of skating to its highest level ever. Skaters didn't jump or spin; instead, they moved rather stiffly and formally around the ice. When a skater was finished, however, a precise and elaborate figure had been etched on a frozen lake for everyone to admire.

When I was still competing as an amateur, skaters were judged on three things: figures and the short and long freestyle programs.

Figures didn't have as much excitement and suspense as freestyle, but they were quite important. They taught body control and concentration. There wasn't much of an audience. Instead, you would show up at a lonely rink and trace and retrace a figure for the judges; the slightest wiggle or wobble meant deductions. Those scores were factored with the scores for the short program and the long program to determine skaters' overall placements. Figures could mean the difference between winning or losing a medal.

Compulsory figures were eliminated in 1991, in part because they didn't make good television, and in part because skaters who excelled at figures could build up huge leads and win over more talented freestyle skaters. At the 1972 Olympic Winter Games, Austria's Beatrix Schuba finished first in figures; America's Janet Lynn finished fourth. Although many experts think that Lynn was one of the best freestyle skaters of all time, she couldn't overtake Schuba's lead to win the gold medal. At the World Championship that same year, Schuba was so far ahead in figures that she won the gold despite the fact that she finished *ninth* in the free skate.

Ladies' figure skating has changed dramatically since figures were eliminated. It takes years to learn figures. You never used to see a fourteen-year-old girl beat a twenty-year-old to win a National or World title. When Kristi Yamaguchi was coming up through the ranks, she'd score low in figures, skate wonderfully and score high in her short and long programs, and only pull up to fifth place. She couldn't win a medal until she mastered figures. Now you're seeing younger and younger skaters winning National and World championships.

A lot of skaters hated practicing compulsory figures and thought they were boring, but I loved figures. It's a real thinker's sport. You're constantly making decisions. For example, in competition, you have a whole strip of clean ice, and you have to decide where to lay out, or place, your figure. You have to decide whether to avoid

hills (slopes in the ice) or use them to your advantage. You have to decide what markings in the ice to use as a guide, and you have to keep your figure from getting confused with another skater's figure. I found that practicing figures provided a quiet, almost meditative challenge and required great concentration.

Under pressure, however, I rarely performed figures as well as I could. I always got too nervous and I would just shake.

Many people say that skaters who had to do figures learned to freeskate better because figures teach you edge control. I feel that figures helped develop discipline, body control, and balance, but not the strength, quickness, and musicality needed for freestyle. The best thing about figures is that they teach you to concentrate, which you can use in other parts of life.

LINDA LEAVER ON COACHING BRIAN

Brian was very coachable. If you asked him to do something, he'd be very open to trying it. He was also very truthful with himself and with me. If he was afraid to do something, he'd say so. That meant that I was always able to deal with the reality of the situation. Not every skater is like that. Often skaters will hide behind excuses, such as blades that are too dull, or cold feet, or tiredness, when the real reason they don't want to try might be fear or shyness.

I never had to push Brian. Ninety percent of the time, he was pulling me. He had a love of skating, of getting better, jumping higher, spinning faster, turning more times, pushing his talent to the limit. He had that drive from the first day; he could spend hours working on his skating. That kind of work ethic is the single most important thing that separates Brian and other super-elite athletes from everyone else.

But when he was young, I don't think *he* thought he was working! He was the first one on the ice and the last one off. The only skating session he ever missed was the Saturday morning after his senior prom. He stayed up all night and fell asleep just before he was supposed to get up the next morning.

One of the hardest things about competitive skating—and coaching—is getting up early. If you want to get good practice ice, you have to be at the rink when other people don't want to be there. For us, that was 5:30 A.M. And when you spend six hours straight on the ice, you get very cold.

The United States Figure Skating Association gave me some money when I was a novice to help pay skating expenses. In my thank-you letter (above) I outlined the goals that I had set for myself at thirteen. A year later, I was on my way; I came in third at the World Junior Championships (right).

Dear Mr. Roy Winder,

I have entered many competitions since I started skating at eight and a half. Skating is very exciting and the people involved in skating are very helpful and friendly. I enjoy skating because I have fun practicing and learning new things.

My main ambition in figure skating is to be the National, World, and Olympic champion for the United States. I know it will take a lot of work and practice to achieve this goal but I am willing to work hard and put in a tremendous amount of effort. Thank You

Brian
Boitano

Ｆamous COACHES AND THEIR STUDENTS

Some coaches have trained so many students to national and world medals that they're almost as famous as their skaters. For example:

Richard Callaghan coached Nicole Bobek, and now coaches Todd Eldredge and Tara Lipinski.

Frank Carroll coached Linda Fratianne, Tiffany Chin, Christopher Bowman, and now coaches Michelle Kwan.

Carlo Fassi coached Robin Cousins, John Curry, Peggy Fleming, Dorothy Hamill, Caryn Kadavy, and Jill Trenary.

Coach Frank Carroll helps Michelle Kwan with a position.

Ron Ludington coached Kitty & Peter Carruthers, along with many other national and international pairs champions.

Gustave Lussi coached Dick Button and Dorothy Hamill.

Jutta Muller coached Jan Hoffmann, Anett Pötzsch, and Katarina Witt.

John Nicks coached Tai Babilonia & Randy Gardner, JoJo Starbuck & Kenneth Shelley, Kristi Yamaguchi & Rudy Galindo, and Jenni Meno & Todd Sand.

Mary and Evy Scotvold coached David Santee, Nancy Kerrigan, and Paul Wylie.

Tatiana Tarasova coached Irina Rodnina with Alexei Ulanov and with Alexandr Zaitsev, Natalia Bestemianova & Alexander Bukin, Oksana Grishuk & Evgeni Platov, Irina Slutskaya, and Ilia Kulik.

Galina Zmievskaya coached Viktor Petrenko and Oksana Baiul.

Dave Black

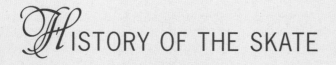

HISTORY OF THE SKATE

One of the oldest pairs of skates in the world was found at an excavation on the banks of Lake Moss in Switzerland. Scientists estimate these, and others, were made around 3,000 B.C.—which means skating has been around for almost 5,000 years.

Many other early skates have been uncovered in Europe, the British Isles, and especially throughout Scandinavia, where it is believed that early people first began to use a form of skating as a means of transportation and hunting on the frozen lakes and rivers.

The first skates were made from bone—the leg, jaw, and rib bones of large animals like horses, reindeer, and elk. The bones were polished and sharpened, holes were bored through each end, and leather straps threaded through the holes were tied around the feet. The bottoms of the bones were greased with lard to help the skaters move. Of course, they couldn't glide the way people do today, so they used long pointed poles, similar to cross-country ski poles, to push themselves along.

The Dutch are generally credited with further developments of the skate blade. By the early fourteenth century, carved wooden skates were popular, though they were wide and clumsy and could not hold their sharpness. Iron strips were then embedded into the wood to give a smoother running edge.

About 1550, a blacksmith, supposedly by mistake, made a narrow iron blade that proved capable of easier control and maneuvering. These blades were developed and refined so that the hand-forged iron blades had large curled prows to cut through the snow. They attached to wooden platforms with a screw or spike that went into the boot's heel to hold it in place, with the toe and ankle tied to the platform with thongs. With sharp edges that dug into the ice, skaters could throw away their poles. They learned to push off with one foot and glide on the other, alternating feet, to travel from town to town on Holland's frozen canals. This skating style was called "the Dutch roll."

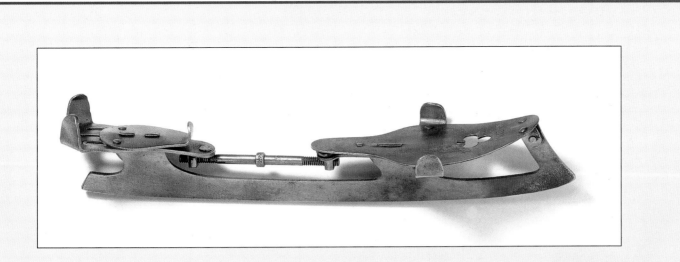

Skating spread throughout Europe and was brought to Great Britain by the royal family as both transportation and recreation. In 1837, Henry Boswell, an Englishman, invented "fluted skates," adding a groove down the middle to give them the inside and outside edges that skaters still use today, and shortened the length for increased maneuverability, speed, and quick turns.

An American, E.V. Bushnell, made the first all steel skate in 1870, with adjustable clamps that clipped the skate onto the skater's boot and did away with the sometimes painful straps. A skating craze swept America and by the late 1870s, more than two hundred patents for designs had been issued.

Skates with little teeth on the front, called "rake skates," came to the United States from Sweden. John Martin of Massachusetts then added a single spike, called a "diamond point," on the front of the blade in 1867, to allow for pirouettes, spins, and other moves. By 1900 skaters could buy blades permanently attached to the boots, much as we know them today.

I own a few pairs of antique skates that I found in antique stores or that friends gave me. The oldest pair (opposite page) dates from the 1800s. I would have loved to see someone skate with these blades; compared to today's blades, it would have been very tough.

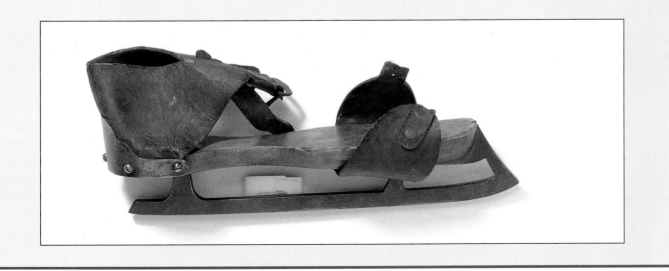

$\mathscr{M}$Y TRAINING REALLY BEGAN
when I started taking private lessons. When I was in elementary school, my mom would pick me up at 2:30 P.M., take me to the rink, and I'd skate until 8:00 P.M. Then I'd go home, do homework, and go to bed.

In high school, my schedule switched around. I'd get out of bed at 4:30 A.M. and I'd be at the rink at 5:30 A.M. I'd skate until 10:00 A.M. and then go to school. I missed the first two periods, but that was okay because they were physical education and a free period, and I received P.E. credit for skating. I was lucky, because my teachers and principal supported my skating and helped me organize my schedule. Otherwise, I wouldn't have had enough practice time.

(Opposite page) I proudly show off an interclub competition trophy with two of my best skating friends, Susie Steindorf (middle) and Susie Prestin (right).

After another competition, all the medalists from my club mug for a local newspaper photographer (right). I led the line and, in my enthusiasm, accidentally kicked the kid behind me.

When skaters start competing at an elite level, some choose to take correspondence classes and have tutors rather than go to school. I didn't do that because I thought it was important to attend school and be with other kids my own age. Not everyone spends every waking moment discussing triple toe loops!

I made great friends at the rink, mostly girls. In fact, my first kiss was on the ice. I was about eight or nine, and most of the girls were older. They all thought I was cute, so they'd kiss me all the time.

I always looked forward to summer because I would spend almost the whole day practicing with my friends. We'd skate from 7:45 A.M. until noon and then have a half-hour break. We'd go in a group across the street to the 7-Eleven for microwaved burritos and Slurpees, then we'd come back to the rink and skate from 12:30 to 2 P.M. We gave each other nicknames, basically the goofiest names we could think of, like Eunice and Elroy. My nickname was Seymour.

Later, when I was fourteen, I started training at a rink that had rats running around—and they were big rats, too! We'd be skating at 5:30 A.M. and we'd look up and see the rats walking along the ceiling girders. One time my friend Lisa and I were standing at the boards talking and a huge rat fell off a girder and landed right next to her.

I took off. Lisa later claimed that I actually pushed her toward the rat in my attempt to escape—but that's not true. I did skate faster than I ever had in my life.

There used to be about twenty skaters on the ice for each practice session and I remember endless arguments over what kind of music to play during the warm-ups. One group of kids would want Top 40 and another group would want punk rock. By the time they finished arguing, the ten-minute warm-up would be over and no one got to listen to any music.

To this day, those skating friends are some of the best friends I've ever had. Sometimes I wish I could go back to that time.

Part of what made the experience so wonderful was working with Linda. She was a great coach. I started with her when I was eight years old, and we're still working together, over twenty-five years later. She had weekly contests for her students. We might have a sit spin contest, to see who could spin the longest without falling over. Or

Linda's students threw a surprise birthday party for her every year—and she always acted surprised! I'm on the far right, eagerly watching her unwrap her present.

(Opposite page) We always had a lot of fun at out-of-town competitions. Here I am hanging out with Susie Prestin and Susie Steindorf on Puget Sound, where we were skating in an interclub competition.

BREAKING IN BOOTS

I love new boots, but not breaking them in. The leather is stiff and unyielding, so they're difficult to skate in. It takes weeks for new boots to form to your feet and be comfortable. I begin breaking them in off the ice before the blades are mounted.

First, I put them on the floor and fill them with hot water. During this breaking in process, I get a lot of cuts and scrapes on my ankles and feet, so I pad my boots with silicone or foam rubber. I walk around and bend them for a week, about a half hour each time. Then the blades are mounted and I skate in them. After I make that move into new boots, my old boots feel like slippers.

I try to change my boots once a year. I break them in during the first part of the season and then I have them rebuilt, so they're strong through the whole season.

Rebuilding means gluing new leather in the interior, to make it stronger. The boots are stiff, but they'll still bend, because they've been broken in. That's when boots are perfect.

we'd play "add-on." That's where one skater will do a move, like a double toe loop, then the next skater will do that move plus one more, like a double toe loop plus a loop or a walley. Each skater adds on a move until someone finally misses.

When I was a kid, I hung out with Linda all the time, not just at the rink. Linda's husband went to Stanford University and they lived in an old abandoned college dormitory. On weekends, she'd have her students come over, and we'd run around and play hide-and-seek in the empty dorm rooms. Later, as a teen, I used to ride my bike over to her house to see what they were having for dinner, or to play on her trampoline.

Sometimes Linda would take a few of her students on trips to compete and train with more advanced skaters. I remember staying at a Rodeway Inn in Seattle when I was competing in the preliminary boys' division of the Puget Sound interclub competitions. Once Linda piled us all in her car and drove to Los Angeles to watch the top U. S. skaters train. When I was thirteen, several of us spent three weeks one summer training in Sun Valley, Idaho. That was great because we got to see great skaters from all over the country who were competing at a level or two higher than we were. We'd see what kind of moves they were doing and it would inspire us to work even harder.

When my friend Yvonne Gomez and I were both training with Linda, we could get really goofy. We were serious about training, but we also laughed all the time. Looking back, it's hard to describe what was so funny. We were just always joking, the way friends do.

One time, Linda told us that her mother had visited Scotland and had seen the castle that had belonged to their ancestors. So for the rest of the session, Yvonne and I called her "milady" and bowed or curtsied any time she asked us to do something.

Linda also always listened to me. I think that's a really important thing for a coach to do, because kids definitely have an idea of how they want to do things and what works best for them. In my case, I was always too hard on myself, but Linda was good at pumping me up. If I had a bad day, she'd say, "It's going to be okay, you can do

Linda watches as I work on my figures during a practice session at the 1987 U.S. Nationals. She's wearing furry boots to keep her feet warm. She didn't wear skates because her blades would mark up the ice where I was skating my figures.

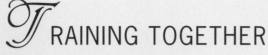

TRAINING TOGETHER

Yvonne and I practiced figures for three and a half hours a day while training. We concentrated so hard that we had to take breaks once in a while and tell jokes, just to relax a little.

For six years, Yvonne Gomez and I were both coached by Linda Leaver. We trained together, laughed together, cried together and, in the end, went to the Olympics together. Yvonne had a dual citizenship in the United States and Spain, so she competed for Spain.

I always say that I'd like to create a TV sitcom based on Yvonne's life. She always has some funny story to tell, like the time she skated in a competition and found out that her music had been recorded twenty seconds too fast. She had to skate her whole program like a whirling dervish—but she finished.

I've known Brian for fifteen or twenty years. Even before we started training together, we went to the same competitions and knew each other. He competed at a level above me, and I always thought he was a great skater.

We really became buddies when I was sixteen years old. At that time, I had another coach and was taking one lesson a week from Linda. She didn't really want another student, but Brian convinced her to take me on. He wanted to train with someone who was as serious as he was. I also think he wanted companionship.

We spent five to seven hours at the rink together every day. We didn't socialize much after practice; in fact, we barely got through the day, then went home and crashed. Tired is a good way to describe those years—tired and hungry. But they were also great years. We laughed so much.

I remember the summer that Brian and I went to France to train with a coach who was an expert in figures. I went to a French elementary school, so I have a decent understanding of the language. Brian didn't know that—and for some reason I was too shy to speak. So for a couple of days, I just watched as Brian struggled to communicate with people. Finally, I got so frustrated watching him play charades that I started speaking French. I'll never forget the look he gave me! He was so mad—but it was worth it, just to see the look on his face!

We shared a little studio apartment while we were in France. It was so tiny, I had to crawl over his bed to get to mine. The kitchen was part of the living room, which was part of the bathroom. Brian had to make a shower curtain out of garbage bags to keep the water from flooding the apartment. We ate rice cakes all summer long, because we were always dieting, but we had a wonderful time.

It was great having Brian around, especially as we got ready for a competition. Training at that time is so incredibly tense. You know you're about to perform in front of thousands of people, all by yourself on the ice, sometimes doing jumps that you're only fifty-fifty on. There's nothing else in my life that has come close to that feeling of pressure, so there was a lot of talking and crying and laughing and occasionally some yelling. We ran through the whole range of emotions.

But we could support each other without even talking. Sometimes I'd have a bad day in practice and I'd be really upset. Brian would just give me a look, and I knew that he was saying, "I know how you feel, but get your act together. You can do it."

He always stood with Linda when I competed to give me emotional support. One time, I was on the ice waiting for my name to be called. I had tendonitis in my ankle and was in a lot of pain. I remember looking over at him, thinking, "Help me. I can't do this." He just gave me a look of complete confidence—it was like he was saying, "Do it. I know you can."—and I went out and skated a perfect performance.

In 1986, my foot hurt so badly that I actually quit skating for a year. Then I decided to go back and try to skate in the Olympics in 1988. I wanted to go to the Olympics with Brian.

On the night of the men's long program at the 1988 Olympics, I was sitting in the stands. The minute Brian took the ice for warm-up, I lost it. I realized that sixteen years of work were coming down to this moment, and the impact of that realization made me start crying. I cried nonstop from that minute to the end of Brian's program when the audience members were on their feet going crazy. I've never cried so much in my life. I didn't even know if he'd won, but I was so proud of him. I ran backstage and on my way I heard someone yell, "Boitano won!"

When I saw him, the first thing he said was, "Thank you for giving up a year for me." I have to say it was one of the best years of my life.

TRAINING DIET

In my late teens, I was taller than everyone else. I was competing with smaller guys and I looked huge in comparison. Because I'm tall for a skater (I'm 5 foot 11 inches), the judges always wanted me to be really, really thin. Female skaters often may find that a lot of attention is paid to their weight, especially after they go through puberty. Their bodies change, they often can't do jumps as well until they re-adjust, and coaches or judges often pressure them to keep their weight down.

It's unusual for male skaters to face that, but some judges told me I was heavy. When you're young and one person tells you something like that, it's like one hundred people telling you. One time I was nibbling on a cracker at a competition when a judge spotted me and came over to say, "You'd better stop, or you're going to get fat."

I was never fat; in fact, I was probably about ten pounds *underweight* when I was competing, so staying thin was always a struggle for me.

I tried different diets, and I always ended up eating what I craved—carbohydrates. So I consulted a nutritionist and came up with a diet based on pastas and breads and crackers.

A good training diet consists of balanced meals with all the food groups every day, so now I also eat a lot of vegetables and fish and avoid fats. I have a sweet tooth for non-fat gummy things, like gummy worms, licorice, and cinnamon bears. Before a competition, I'll eat more small, light meals, but every skater has to find out what works for him.

I did learn, however, that it was more important to stay healthy and do what was best for my body than to meet some judges' unrealistic demands.

it; tomorrow we'll try another approach and it will work."

When a skater looks for a coach, he should try to find a nurturing person, someone he feels a connection with. He should feel that his coach is helping him to be his best —and he should never feel scared of his coach.

Some skaters like coaches who push to motivate them. The coach will yell, "Come on, get going, get going, get going." But there's a fine line between doing that and yelling, "You can't do it, you're too lazy and you're too dumb." Skaters who have those kind of coaches never seem to have any confidence. They don't do well in competition, maybe because they feel that their coaches won't like them if they make mistakes, which puts them under too much pressure.

Today, most of my off-ice training is meant to keep my knees healthy. I ride my bike and do slideboard. I never took dance, but a lot of skaters do, especially the Russians. Dance classes can help if you don't have a natural fluid movement on the ice or if you want to be more limber. I've done some weight lifting, but in general I think that hurts your skating. Skaters have to be quick and agile in their upper bodies to do jumps. If you get bulky and muscular, you lose that quickness.

And when skaters try to learn a jump, quickness and timing are everything. They start by learning the single jumps, then build off those single jumps to learn the doubles and triples. The first thing a skater does is just fling himself into the air and fall. Skaters can't see anything when they're turning in the air; it's all feel. They have to learn the feel of the momentum coming into the jump, the timing in the air, and what works.

Once the jump feels right, the skater repeats it over and over until it is good enough to place in a program to music. I always used the same timing, speed, and pattern across the ice to develop consistency.

I'd work on jump positions and rotation in the air on Linda's trampoline. I experimented with different flying sit spin positions, too, but it didn't really mimic the feeling of the speed and edges you have on the ice.

The same thing holds true for practicing jumps in a harness. I know that works for a lot of skaters, but I always felt the set-up wasn't realistic enough. You put on a harness that goes across the rink to keep you from

During a practice session, I prepare to take off in a triple Axel. Someday I think a skater will land a quintuple jump (five revolutions), but I don't think they'll ever be commonplace. Of course, Linda's coach used to tell her that women would never do triples!

COLD HARD CASH

It costs a lot of money for a skater to train at the national and international level—as much as $50,000 a year, at last count. That includes custom-made boots at $600 a pair, blades at $400 to $500 a pair, coaching fees of $100 an hour and up, costume costs of $700 and up per outfit, plus practice time at the rink, and travel, hotel, and food costs for the skater, coach, and family members when competition time rolls around.

Fortunately, restrictions on earning money as an amateur have been relaxed quite a bit in the last few years, which helps today's skaters cover part of their training costs. When I was competing, a skater could be disqualified from amateur competition for receiving a gift of more than twenty-five dollars, or for earning any money for figure skating, whether the payment was for appearing in an exhibition or giving a lesson. Today, amateur skaters are allowed to earn money by going on tour and some major competitions offer prize money.

First quadruple jump: Kurt Browning (Canada) landed a quadruple toe loop at the 1988 World Championships. He was spinning at 300 revolutions per minute.

This time-lapse photo of my quadruple toe loop was taken between midnight and 5 A.M. in a pitch-black rink. Sixteen cameras were lined up on the ice; I had to jump in a five-foot square area directly in front of them. Each time I jumped, sixteen flashes would go off in an instant; then the darkness would return and I would get ready to jump again.

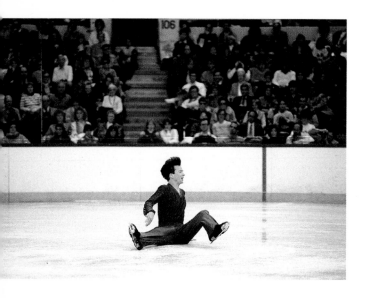

falling, but you can't get any speed leading into the jump and you can't follow your normal pattern of approaching the jump.

I probably fell tens of thousands of times during the years that I was learning jumps. I'd fall between ten and twenty times a lesson. I had bruises on my hip and I was stiff and sore the next day, but I'd want to try again anyway. When I was really young, I'd stuff Styrofoam in my pants to cushion my falls. A lot of girls wore "crash pads" over their dresses to cushion their falls.

Longest jump: Robin Cousins (England) jumped nineteen feet, one inch performing an Axel.

Longest spin: Nathalie Kreig (Switzerland) spun for three minutes and twenty seconds.

Fastest spinner: Ronald Robertson (USA) could spin up to 240 rotations a minute.

Sometimes when skaters watch each other, they can feel in their own bodies what another skater is doing. When someone has a bad fall—falls on his tailbone or his legs go splat on the ice—I can feel it through my own body. Sometimes when I see a skater leaning too far in the air and I know a bad fall is coming, I turn away. I can't even watch.

Learning spins can be difficult, too. Skaters have to learn to spin fast, stay in one spot on the ice, and look good while they're doing it. It's hard to learn good positions, such as sitting all the way down in a sit spin or holding your extended leg even with or higher than your head on a camel spin.

People always wonder if I get dizzy when I spin, or if I get used to it. The answer is yes, all skaters get dizzy and no, they never get completely used to it—they just learn how to deal with the dizziness. I learned to focus on a spot on the wall or look down at the ice after a spin, until I wasn't dizzy any more. When planning a program, experienced skaters know to not put a jump right after a spin!

I can probably spin for forty-five seconds or longer if I change positions and change feet. When skaters change feet, they push off with each change of foot. That gives more momentum and the spin lasts longer.

Great competitive skaters have to learn how to do all the technical elements—the jumps, the spins, the footwork—and they

I successfully defended my title at the 1986 U.S. National Championships, despite a fall on my triple flip (above left). The secret to competition is not letting mistakes take over. You have to fight the whole way through.

SPEED IS WHAT I NEED

No wonder it's sometimes hard to tell if a skater just did a double or a triple Lutz: jumps are completed in just one second. In that fraction of a moment, a skater will jump about 26 inches off the ice and travel about ten feet. When preparing to take off for a jump, a skater may travel as fast as 15 miles an hour.

A top skater will complete as many as six spin rotations in one second, and seventy rotations in a single spin. Ronnie Robertson, the 1956 Olympic silver medalist and one of the greatest spinners ever, once appeared on TV and demonstrated that he could spin faster than an electric fan!

DREAMS AND NIGHTMARES

I used to have skating nightmares. I'd dream that the announcer said, "Representing the United States, Brian Boitano." I'd think, "I don't have my costume on. I don't have my skates on. I'm not ready!" Or I'd dream that I went on the ice with the wrong blades, or wearing someone else's boots.

I used to remember all my dreams, but that stopped after the 1988 Olympics. Now, I'm just beginning to remember my dreams again. I think that's because the concentrated

pressure of the Olympics takes years off your life. It's two weeks in a highly concentrated state where you have to focus and push away a lot of negativity. I felt that I was sapped of every bit of energy and I needed to rest for the next decade.

I also found it hard to do visualizations after the Olympics. It was like I expended all my energy on that one moment.

I used visualization a lot when I was competing as an amateur. Visualization involves closing your eyes and imagining something you want to happen with as much sensory detail—including sights, sounds, smells, and feelings—as possible. However, when I tried to visualize my actual skating, I'd see myself missing things. So most of the time, I'd imagine the feeling I got when I did my program perfectly. I'd picture myself going into the jump and then feeling exactly how I wanted to feel on the landing. I wanted to feel like, "Yes, I'm doing really well."

I mentally went through my figures, my short program, my long program—I even visualized standing on the podium and listening to "The Star-Spangled Banner."

In fact, the night I won the Olympic gold medal, everything happened exactly how I'd visualized it: the way I cried at the end of my program and then laughed, and the way the audience stood before I was done. I actually started thinking, "Is this real or am I visualizing it?"

It wasn't until I was standing on the podium and "The Star-Spangled Banner" began to play that I realized that I had really won. The music played at a faster tempo than I had visualized and I thought, "This is too fast." Then I thought, "But this is real. It's real!"

also have to learn how to compete. There's no secret to doing a good job in competition: I always made every practice simulate a competition as closely as I could. I'd warm up the same way I would in a competition, then I'd give myself one chance to do the program. After that, I'd work on sections of the program for the rest of the practice, concentrating on correcting any mistakes.

I was very hard on myself when I was young. If I made one mistake in my long program, I felt as if I'd had a horrible day. If I made *two* mistakes, it was catastrophic. When I went home, I would just be living for the next day when I could go back to the rink and prove to myself that I could do my program flawlessly.

As much as I hated making mistakes, I very rarely stopped the music and started over. If I didn't learn how to deal with a mistake during practice, then falling during competition would really shake my confidence. Sometimes skaters forget their programs or become disoriented on the ice after a fall. They may find themselves thinking, "Where am I? What am I doing?"

That's why it's important to go through programs in practice without stopping and make the best of your errors, because you never know what's going to happen in competition.

Japan's Midori Ito experienced an extreme—and extremely unusual—accident during the 1991 World Championships. She was skating so close to the boards that she actually jumped out of the rink and almost knocked over a TV camera! She kept smiling, stepped back onto the ice, finished her program—and ended up in fourth place. That's grace under pressure!

Some skaters do their program several times in a row without stopping in order to build up their stamina. I think practicing programs when you're exhausted can actually teach you to make and expect mistakes.

The only way to get confidence in a competitive setting is to have a backlog of good performances during practice. That's what helps you through a pressure situation. By the time I get on the ice to compete, I've practiced that program for a year. I've done it hundreds of times, so there's not really a chance of forgetting it. Sometimes I even go through my program in my dreams!

HIGHS AND LOWS

My worst competition was the 1994 Winter Olympics in Lillehammer. After winning the gold medal in 1988, I had thought, "I'm not done." So I competed for five years as a professional, then had the opportunity to reinstate as an amateur and try for a third Olympics.

I felt that I could still compete technically, so I thought, "Why not?"

I was plagued with knee injuries that whole year and practiced in pain. But the amazing thing was that my knee never hurt in competition. My doctor said that the adrenaline from competition dulled the pain. I made my third Olympic team and was in really great shape.

Then I made an uncharacteristic mistake in the short program at the Olympics and lost any chance of winning a medal.

I thought that people would be disappointed in me for losing in 1994. But instead they gave me credit for my effort. When I went on tour afterward, the audience response was incredible. It was as if they completely understood my need for a challenge, my disappointment, the fact that I couldn't be perfect all the time—and they still liked my skating.

My best competition—other than the 1988 Olympics—was the 1986 World Championships. I had tendonitis in my ankle. The pain was excruciating; I could hardly walk, let alone skate. However, my doctor said that I couldn't cause any further damage by skating, so I decided to compete.

I think you can endure pain if you know that you're not causing permanent damage. I didn't even tape my ankle when I skated, because I wanted to be in control of it.

Winning that competition taught me how powerful the mind can be. I thought, "If I can make my body do what I want it to do when it hurts this much, just imagine what I can do when I'm healthy." I think that experience was a stepping stone to winning the 1988 Olympics.

$\mathscr{L}$INDA LEAVER ON TRAINING

I consult with Linda during a practice session at a competition, asking her what moves need more work or what other things I should practice during my time on the ice.

When you learn to skate, you develop your motion memory. That's a complex memory of a physical action that's often described as a feeling. The more developed your motion memory, the better you can repeat the movement and describe its different parts.

For example, when you first learn a jump, you may describe it as feeling like a whir or you may just be aware of pulling in your arms. As your motion memory develops, you become conscious of your body alignment, the placement of your arms, head and legs, how fast you're going, the sounds your blades make, and your timing. This awareness enables you to become consistent. Brian's motion memory is so good that he can be off the ice for weeks and skate flawlessly when he returns. He can also adjust an incorrect move in mid-air.

The harder a jump or move is, the longer it takes to learn. Brian learned all five single-revolution jumps in his first lesson. It took him five more months to learn the more difficult single Axel, which requires an extra half-revolution in the air. Brian's learning process was steady and constant. He fell as many as twenty times a day for months trying to land his difficult triples. It seemed to him like he

wasn't making progress, but by the time he had mastered each jump, he knew exactly how to complete it every time.

Some skaters progress more erratically. They may land their jumps the first time they try them and then not land them again for days. This can be discouraging, but with persistence they will master them. Both ways of learning are okay.

It's the coach's job to teach correct technique. Improper technique can cause a jump to vary every time. Under pressure the skater will have to rely on luck, which puts the skater at a disadvantage.

As a coach, I didn't get on the ice to demonstrate triple jumps—that would have been extremely foolhardy! I could have coached Brian without even putting on my skates, just by standing at the side of the rink and watching what he was doing. I'd observe his attempts at a triple jump, for example, and try to figure out what he was doing wrong and how it could be corrected. The coach's job is to break down each move into parts, so the skater can understand what he has to do. I might demonstrate a shoulder or arm position, or actually move his shoulders or arms into the correct position. Any little problem could send the skater crashing to the ice.

It's also a coach's job to help shape good mental attitudes. For example, a skater can view failure as a negative or a positive. With a good mental attitude, failures can become incredibly efficient learning devices and motivational tools. In a competitive career, skaters will face bad marks, bad luck of the draw, and injuries. You can use such setbacks to make yourself stronger.

One of a coach's most important responsibilities is teaching good sportsmanship. A coach may have to demand that young people congratulate the winner of a competition, even if they're personally disappointed. I think it's important to teach skaters to show respect for their competitors and a sensitivity to others' feelings. When Brian was on the medal stand at the 1988 Olympics, he graciously stepped down and congratulated Brian Orser. He knew that Brian Orser wanted the gold medal as intensely as he had and had worked as hard, and he was aware of how much emotional pain Brian Orser was feeling at that moment.

I believe that skaters should build on their strengths and work on their weaknesses. I didn't want my students to say, "I should have won because I did twice as many triples." Instead, I wanted them to ask, "What did my competitors do that I didn't? Were their jumps higher, were their spins faster, was their program more balanced?" It's important to be strong in all areas: jumps, spins, footwork, style, musicality, presentation, flexibility, speed, strength, power, and stamina, to name just a few.

Skating is an incredibly complicated sport, which is why I love it. It's never boring! Just when you think skating is within your grasp, there's a new area to conquer. When learning jumps, a skater can focus on the footwork leading up to the jump, the entry, the air position; with spins, they work on spinning faster, staying in one spot on the ice, developing beautiful positions, getting lower on sit spins; for footwork, they have to develop more complicated patterns and work on deeper edges. In addition, skaters have to fine-tune the small, aesthetic details, like graceful arm movements or pointed toes, and develop performing skills, like interpreting music and connecting with the audience.

When a skater gets stuck on one thing, there's *always* something else to work on. For example, if Brian is breaking in new boots, he may work on

choreography or spins instead of jumps. Even on bad practice days, when everything seems to be going wrong, you can still accomplish something.

I firmly believe in goal-oriented practices. Some skaters feel they've accomplished something if they practice for a couple of hours; they focus more on the time they've spent on the ice than on what they've done with that time. Brian always practices with a purpose in mind. First, you establish your long-term goal. Then each day you set specific short-term goals and gear your practice session toward accomplishing them. Soon you will be rewarded with progress.

To enjoy skating, you have to enjoy the process—and above all, have fun!

As I practice in my home rink before the 1988 Olympics, I know that years of hard work are about to be put to the test.

Goals to Work on

1. get inside eight and waltz eight good by May

2. get first test passing by April 1st — ready to take in May

3. get consistent axel (OK!!) double salchow, split flip, flying sit

   by interclub in May

4. get wallies in better form and speed — get stroking always

   good, get flying camel good

5. try to get double toe loop and double loop consistent

✻ 6. skate three patches a week minimum until competition, always

   skate your best when you go to other rinks, don't compare

   yourself to the others, just keep trying

When I first started working with Linda, she set goals for me every year like this list from 1978 (inset). Sometimes I wasn't happy to hear that I wasn't doing a certain move well—but I secretly liked knowing whát I needed to focus on. Years later, during the 1994 Olympic year, we were still setting goals.

SKATING SLANG

As in every sport, skaters sometimes speak a language all their own. Here's how to know what they're talking about—or how to sound like a skater yourself.

boards: the wooden barrier at the side of the rink; during competitions, they're usually covered with ads.

butt pad: a pad worn inside practice clothes to cushion falls on the ice.

clean: without mistakes: "I skated a clean program."

deduction: a percentage of a point taken off a skater's final score due to a mistake made while performing in competition.

double/double: a jump combination consisting of two double jumps in a row. (Double/triple is a double jump followed by a triple jump; triple/triple consists of two triple jumps in a row.)

draw: the order in which skaters perform during a competition, chosen by random drawing.

flutz: a jump that's supposed to be a Lutz, but where the skater changes to an inside edge before launching off the toe pick, which turns the jump into the easier flip.

kiss and cry: the area where skaters sit after their programs and wait to see the judges' marks; so-called because skaters usually kiss their coaches and often cry, either because they a) performed poorly; b) performed exceptionally well; or c) are simply overcome with emotion.

long: The four-minute, thirty-second (four minutes for women) program skated by singles and pairs skaters: "I'm feeling really comfortable with my long."

Midori: the act of a skater jumping into or over the boards at rinkside; named after Japan's Midori Ito, who jumped out of the rink and into the camera pit during the 1991 World Championships: "If you keep skating so close to the boards, you'll end up doing a Midori."

miss: fail to complete a jump: "I missed my double Axel."

mop up the ice: fall many times during a program: "She really mopped up the ice at Nationals."

nail: doing a jump successfully: "I nailed my Axel!"

Nationals: the U.S. National Championships: "In another year, I hope to go to Nationals."

over-rotate: Turn more than the required rotations in the air on a jump, so that the blade of the landing foot does not land exactly backward; it can result in anything from a shaky landing, stepping out of the landing, or a fall: "He over-rotated his Axel and fell."

panel: the five to nine people judging your competition: "What's your panel like?"

patch: the session in which skaters practice figures; called that because the figures are done on a small area, or patch, of ice: "Are you going to do patch today?"

place: ranking at the end of a competition: "Where did you place?"

pop: do fewer rotations than planned during a jump; for example, changing a double into a single in mid-air: "I popped my triple Lutz."

practice ice: a certain time during the day when a rink is closed to the public and the ice is reserved for a skater's practice: "The only time I could get practice ice was 5:30 in the morning!"

program: a choreographed routine skated to music (never called a routine): "What music are you using for your program?"

quad: a quadruple jump

rink: the ice arena: "When are you heading to the rink?"

short: The two-minute, forty-second technical program skated by singles and pairs skaters: "How did you do during your short?"

single: turn a multi-revolution jump into a single: "He singled his Axel." Also see *pop*.

skate: a performance or program: "I had a good skate tonight."

step out: stepping out of an over-rotated jump, rather than holding a long, controlled landing: "She landed her double Axel, but she had to step out of it."

take out the flowers: crash into the boards during a competition or show. (In exhibition skating, there might actually be flowers at rinkside that you crash into!)

turn out: a less-than-clean jump landing: "I turned out of my triple flip."

two-foot: landing a jump on two feet rather than one, or tapping down the second foot for balance: "He two-footed his Axel."

under-rotate: make fewer than the required rotations in the air on a jump, resulting in the blade of the landing foot hitting the ice short of backward.

warm-up: a period of time, usually about six minutes, in which skaters are allowed on the ice to warm up their muscles before a competition: "I hit all my jumps in the warm-up, so I feel pretty confident."

waxel: an Axel jump that is botched, either by falling, landing poorly, or popping it.

wipe out: take a bad fall: "He really wiped out on that Axel."

Worlds: the World Championships: "My goal is to go to Worlds."

Zamboni: The machine that smooths and makes the ice; skaters call all ice machines Zambonis, even if they're not made by the Zamboni Company.

Practicing during warm-up at a benefit performance in South Bend, Indiana.

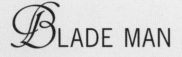LADE MAN

William Craig has sharpened my skates since 1987. He lives in Boston and I live in California, so we actually send blades back and forth across the country via overnight express! Here's what he has to say about the art of blade sharpening:

William Craig prepares to sharpen a blade in his workshop.

Sharpening skate blades isn't high-tech and there are no schools that teach it. It's still a craft—an art form, even. For figure skaters, sharpening is very personal because the blade is the connection between the skaters and the ice. Skaters want that blade to feel the same all the time so they can develop consistency in their skating; they can progress because they know what's under their feet.

Hockey skates are sharpened every four to five hours of ice time, so it's not a big deal if the sharpening is a little off. But a figure skate blade is made of very high-quality steel, so a sharpening lasts for about a month. If the sharpening is off, a skater's performance will also be off for a whole month.

If you've done a perfect sharpening, the blade feels right immediately. The skater doesn't have to compensate for blades that are too dull or too sharp, or for uneven edges. The blade is an extension of the body; you're not putting your blade into the ice, you're putting your foot into the ice.

But consistency is the real key. Even an incorrect sharpening, if it's always done exactly the same way,

will work because the skater will adjust to that incorrect sharpening. I've had skaters ask me to look at their skates right before a major competition. I might see that the sharpening is way off, but I don't dare fix it. They've learned to compensate for that sharpening and any change could hurt their performance.

A skate blade has a groove down the center between the two edges. That's the "hollow" of the blade. When you sharpen a blade, you're deepening that groove; the deeper you cut into the blade, the sharper it feels to the skater. Different sharpenings are not dictated by how sharp the edges are. I can sharpen the edge so that you cut your finger on it, but when you stand on the ice your feet will fly out from under you, because the hollow is not deep enough.

Skaters who still choose to compete in figures should have their blades sharpened with a groove that's almost flat. If you're an intermediate freestyle skater, you need blades with a medium groove. When you graduate to doing harder jumps, you need a deeper groove.

A skater may say to his sharpener, "I need it a little deeper; it's not holding on the ice." On the other hand, if a blade is too sharp, it will stick in the ice when the skater pushes off for his jump. The skater will say the blade feels "sticky," which means the sharpener has made too deep a groove.

The skate blade is not flat on the bottom but has a slight curve called the radius. With hockey blades, you can change the radius to what the skater wants. With figure blades, there are different sizes of radius and you have to buy the radius that makes you feel comfortable.

When skaters start out, they should buy a blade that they can use for figures and freestyle. As they improve, they should buy blades with a bigger bottom toe pick; they need that for higher and more difficult jumps.

I got to know Brian back in 1985 or 1986 when he brought in a pair of figure blades that he needed to have mounted to his boots and sharpened. That was unusual, because figure skaters always go to the same sharpener. That's part of the mystique of blade sharpening. For the next year, he'd come back every few months to have his blades sharpened, but never for a competition.

After he lost his world title in 1987, he sent his blades to me in Boston. I took a close look and saw that the edges were uneven. When skaters stand on their skates, they should be on both edges. If the edges are off and they try to land on the edge that's high, it won't grip the ice as well and they can fall. We thought that he might have had problems at the World Championships because of that. After that, I did all his sharpening.

Most shops sharpen blades only one way. I always listen to the skaters and try to figure out what they want. Skaters can't always explain that, so you have to read between the lines. Brian told me that after getting his blades sharpened, he carried a two-by-four around and used it to dull the

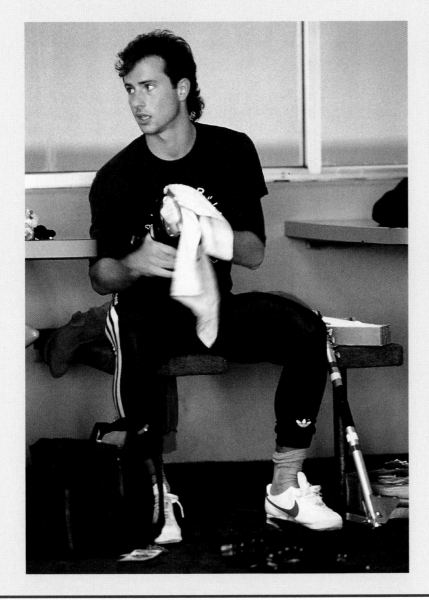

blade to get the feel that he liked! I realized he didn't want his blades crisp. Some skaters can't skate without a razor-sharp edge because they have to jam their blades into the ice and force their jumps. Skaters with a higher level of technical ability, like Brian, often prefer a milder sharpening.

Before the 1988 Olympics in Calgary, we were doing a sharpening a day; the blades were flying back and forth across the country. On the last day, I asked him how his blades felt and he said, "It doesn't matter. I'm ready."

Brian has an exceptionally acute sense of feel. He can sense even tiny differences in the way I sharpen his blades. Over the years, I've developed a routine; I literally count the number of passes I take on Brian's blades when I'm polishing them. If I break from the routine one iota, he can feel it.

One time, I tried to teach someone else to sharpen Brian's skates. I showed him *exactly* how I did it—and Brian could still feel the difference in the "hand," which is the amount of weight I put on the blade as I sharpen and polish it.

Just before the 1994 Olympics in Lillehammer, I finished sharpening his blades, put them in the overnight delivery box at six in the afternoon and shipped them off to California. An hour later, I realized that I had forgotten to make the last two finish passes on the blades. I knew they wouldn't feel right to Brian. So I grabbed the red-eye flight, drove straight to the rink, made a couple of passes on the blade and everything was all right.

If a skater does well in competition, the sharpener is fabulous. If the skater falls flat on his face, the sharpener is often the target for blame. Parents will come to me and say, "My daughter can't do her Axel—or her bunny hop—because the sharpening's not right." When Brian wins a championship, I do have some sense of satisfaction. But I could give those blades to any skater—he's the one who does something exceptional with them.

WHAT'S ON YOUR FEET?

I wear really thin, thin, thin socks when I skate. Some girls wear tights or nylons and some guys wear athletic socks, but I like my foot to be tight in the boot and to be able to feel the ice under me. Some people even go barefoot in their boots.

mark X on tracing, indicating the position, as near as possible, of any corn, bunion or other mal-
, giving particulars below. All remarks shall be given our most careful attention. Photos are helpful.

2 extra cross grind passes

TRACE LEFT FOOT HERE

Blue - old #1
Red - New #3

Brian prefers feeling on old blade

3 passes extra

Left

Hartlick shipped these blades to

#1 R - Take down front of radius
    L - Pick too low, front of radius

#2 R - Radius OK.   Holes OK
    L - Radius OK

    L - 2 passes between toe & ball
    R - a few passes mid to ½ ball & toe

SHARPENING TIPS

Here are a few things skaters should know about having their blades sharpened:

♦ Sharpeners should never change the blade's original radius.

♦ The heel of the blade should remain square and not be rounded off.

♦ The front of the blade should have a nice round arc from the toe picks to the blade. You should never see a lump there; that makes spinning, jump takeoffs and any other move done off the front of the blade more difficult.

♦ The bottom toe pick should never be clipped off. People often trip over that toe pick when they're learning how to skate, so they'll go into their skate shop and ask to have it taken off. That's wrong. The picks force skaters to skate on the center of the blade, under the ball of the foot, for balance. Without toe picks, skaters will skate too far forward on the blade.

♦ The only part of the blade that's tempered steel is the bottom eighth of an inch. Above that is soft steel that won't hold an edge. If blades are so old that they're worn about three-quarters of the way through that tempered steel, you need to buy new blades. When skaters have worn a blade down that far, the bottom toe pick is oversized in comparison with a new blade. When they get new blades, there will be a period of adjustment because they'll feel as if the toe picks are tiny.

♦ How often skates should be sharpened depends on the skater. Competitive skaters who are on the ice five or six days a week usually have their blades sharpened every month, although skaters who like a super sharp edge may go every two weeks. It also depends on the ice you're using. Hockey ice is hard and brittle, while figure skating ice is softer. The harder the ice, the more often you may need to have your blades sharpened.

♦ For competitive skaters, the best time to buy new boots and blades is in late summer. By the time the winter season starts, they both feel comfortable and will be in the best shape for Regionals, Sectionals, and Nationals. At the end of the competitive season, they'll still be in decent enough shape to last you through the summer—and then you buy new ones and start all over again.

♦ Normally skaters should have their blades sharpened five to seven days before they leave for a competition. Then they have a couple of days to skate and make sure the blades feel okay, plus a little time to wear in the blade.

My skate sharpener, William Craig, keeps detailed notes on every blade I use and how it feels (top left). He also makes patterns of every blade (right), which he keeps on file and refers to when sharpening a new blade. The Harlick boot company put an American flag on my boots for good luck before the 1988 Olympics, and has continued to do so ever since.

H - Old 1994 Favorite
From Harlick

A New Blade for 95
Harlick

𝒲HEN SKATERS BEGIN, THEY FOCUS primarily on learning the technical side of the sport. Once they've mastered that, however, they turn their attention to the artistic aspects of skating.

Competing on a national and international level requires a complete package. Skating, choreography, music, costume—the judges look at everything. They may not take specific deductions for an ugly outfit or a bizarre musical choice, but those factors do make a difference. If judges like all the pieces of a program, they'll give the skater better marks.

That's why the decision to consult a choreographer named Sandra Bezic in 1987 turned out to be one of the most important and dramatic changes I made to my skating. At that time, my major competition was Brian Orser of Canada and Alexandr Fadeev from the Soviet Union. They're both small guys and their skating styles were quick and fast, with fast footwork and quick crossovers. I thought I had to do what they did, but better, in order to beat them.

But I'm a big skater and small, quick movements looked better on Orser and Fadeev. So Linda and I went to Sandra for help. She told me, "You have to find out what *you* do best, not try to imitate the other guys."

She suggested that I play up my size and strength. We decided to focus on long, strong lines that would look masculine and heroic. I started to emphasize powerful skating and simple but grand moves, like the spread eagle. It was a dramatic change. I finally felt that I had my own style and that I was comfortable on the ice. I felt, in fact, as if I'd finally come home.

I stayed with my choreographer, Sandra Bezic, and her husband for a couple of weeks when she was choreographing my 1988 Olympic program. Not only do we love working together, but we formed a bond during that time leading up the Olympics that will never be broken.

First skater to skate to music: Jackson Haines (USA) in the mid-1800's.

WHY SKATERS DON'T FALL OVER WHEN PERFORMING A SPREAD EAGLE

When skaters lean back into a spread eagle, it looks as if they should topple over onto the ice. However, centrifugal force—which is defined as the force exerted on a body that is rotating around an axis; it's what you feel when speeding around a tight turn in a roller coaster—pushes out against the skater and lets him lean back and still grip the ice with his skate blades. The faster the skater moves and the tighter the circle, the greater the lean. Fifteen years of experience made the difference between the spread eagle I did when I was nine (inset) and the one I did the year after winning the Olympic gold medal.

Sandra and I spent about six hours a day for three weeks choreographing Carmen on Ice.

When Sandra and I work together to create a program, we have private ice, so it's just the two of us. We'll work for four or five hours straight. Sometimes her husband will bring us coffee and muffins, but we never really stop for a break.

I love working at night. The rink lights are on and the music we're using will be playing on a boom box, but other than that, it's very peaceful. No one else is around. The guy who drives the Zamboni is usually asleep in the office. I find that being alone like that is a great working atmosphere.

When we arrive at the rink to choreograph a program, we start out blank. We don't talk about it ahead of time. As we play the music, Sandra or I will try a certain move. Then we'll stop the tape and work on the move a little, then start the music and try it out again. I'll watch her do something, then I'll repeat the move but add a little

change. Or I'll do a move and she'll tweak it in some way.

As Sandra and I work together on the ice, we talk about the character I'm creating for the program. We often create moves based on these discussions. For example, I skated my long program at the 1994 Olympics to *Appalachian Spring*, by Aaron Copland. The music draws on classic American themes, so we decided that my character would be a pioneer who was settling this new land. At one point, I did a spread eagle sequence from one end of the rink to the other, a move that represented the pioneer surveying his land.

In my short program at the 1988 Olympics, I skated to *Les Patineurs*; my character was based on skaters from a century ago who would etch elaborate patterns in the ice and thrill onlookers with daring jumps and spins. With this character in mind, Sandra made a brilliant suggestion: After I completed my most difficult move, the triple Axel-double loop combination, she said I should reach down, wipe my blade with my hand, and flick the snow over my shoulder, as if to say, "That was easy." The gesture was a little cocky, a little arrogant—just what a supremely confident skater might do on a frozen pond after executing a particularly great move.

For my long program at the 1988 Olympics, I portrayed a soldier. We divided the music into five sections, each portraying a different section of the soldier's life. The program started with the soldier marching resolutely off to war, followed by a section that reflected the soldier's doubts in the aftermath of battle. Next came a waltz section, in which the soldier—now a handsome, romantic hero—was dancing at a ball. This was followed by a segment in which the soldier showed his true self—his vulnerable, loving side—that existed beneath the different personas. The last section was, of course, a victory march.

The day before I skated this program at the Olympics, Sandra suggested one further refinement. Near the end of the program, I performed a spread eagle. As I came out of that move, the music changed to drum beats, signaling the beginning of the victory march segment. Sandra told me

Sandra Bezic choreographed my 1994 Olympic long program (opposite page) to Appalachian Spring *by Aaron Copland. During practice I'd ask Linda about when I needed to work on technically, then consult with Sandra about what I needed to practice artistically (right).*

THE WORD CHOREOGRAPHY MEANS. . .

Choreography is the art of composing the movements, steps, and patterns of a dance. In figure skating, the choreographer must know how skaters move on the ice in order to help the skater interpret the music through movement.

$\mathscr{S}$ANDRA BEZIC ON CHOREOGRAPHY

World-renowned choreographer and former Canadian champion skater Sandra Bezic has created programs for skaters such as Kristi Yamaguchi, Kurt Browning, Katarina Witt, and many others. Some of her most famous programs include Browning's "Casablanca" program at the 1993 World Championship; Lu Chen's 1996 short and long programs to "Spring Breeze" and Rachmaninoff's Piano Concerto No. 2; Yamaguchi's hip and contemporary program to the techno song "Doop Doop"; and Barbara Underhill and Paul Martini's passionate skate to "When a Man Loves a Woman." Here's what she has to say about her work:

As a choreographer, I have to establish the goal of the program and match the music to the skater's personality. Sometimes the goal is to achieve something the skater hasn't ever done before. Perhaps a young skater isn't good at footwork, so you choose music that forces him to work on that. But if the goal is to win an Olympic gold medal, you focus on strengths, not weaknesses.

A choreographer tries to inspire skaters on a daily basis by helping choose music that they can feel in their soul. Once we have the music, I get on the ice with the skater and start working on the program. It's often like a musical jam session, only we're working with physical movements. Sometimes we don't even speak. The skater will do a movement, I'll watch and then repeat it with a slight change, he'll repeat what I did, then I add another movement, and so on.

Choreographing a program takes as much or as little time as you have. It's different for singles skaters and pairs, too. On average, I'd say I spend two hours for each minute of choreography.

A competitive program needs to be blocked out to make competitive sense. You have to include all

the required movements, set the jumps up properly and place them where you know the skater can land them, and give the skater enough recovery time before the next jump. You don't want to have the skater do a triple Lutz at a moment when there's a big crescendo in the music. You're really setting yourself up with such a dramatic musical moment, and then it's almost funny if the skater falls.

You also try to place moves where they'll look best from the judges' point-of-view. The skater shouldn't plan to perform a spin that she does poorly right smack in front of the judges, but sometimes placing it too far away also attracts attention. The best strategy is to put it in a nondescript place and surround it with other strengths.

The biggest mistake young skaters make is thinking that they must have a choreographer. Most coaches are perfectly capable of choreographing a program and they know what their skater needs to learn. It's more important to first learn how to skate. Once your technical ability is solid, then you should think about hiring a choreographer.

Choreographer Sandra Bezic created Kurt Browning's "Casablanca" program (opposite page, top) and Lu Chen's "Spring Breeze" program (opposite page, bottom) as well as Carmen on Ice *(above).*

to pretend that I was marching down the street after having won the war. You should have your nose in the air, she said, because you're proud of having emerged victorious.

I guess I overdid it a little. Jim McKay, the television announcer, even chuckled a little at that part because I looked *so* proud and arrogant.

Sandra often adds those kind of little touches that push me to show my emotions. At one point, she said to me, "You have to be willing to show yourself and your feelings when you skate." A perfect example of choreography that helped me do that was the program she created for me right after the Olympics. The music was an Italian love song called "Parlami d'amore, Mariu," which means "Speak to Me of Love, Mariu." It's sung by Luciano Pavarotti, and of all the music I've ever skated to, it's my favorite.

We worked on the program through the night. We finally finished it in the wee hours of the morning and Sandra asked me to skate the program through one time.

When I finished, I skated over to the rail and saw that Sandra was crying. She pointed to her tears and said, "Look what you did to me." That was really something, for me to move someone I respect so much.

Sandra and I always joke that I'm a tortured soul and that any character who suffers—like Don José, the character I played in *Carmen on Ice*—is perfect for me.

Different performance styles work for different skaters. Some skaters do a lot of posing and staring at the judges during their programs. Some skaters can work an audience—pointing to them and waving to make them cheer back. I try to reach the whole audience. I want to move people, to have them feel my emotions through my skating.

As a professional, I choreograph some of my programs by myself. For example, I created a routine to a Frank Sinatra song called "More." I settled on that piece after listening to a lot of music. I liked the song: it was very cool and relaxed and lounge-lizardy, with a great ending. I thought it was time for me to do something kick-back, not so serious and deep.

I wanted to add some comedy without being too obvious. I hate literal choreography that spells everything out for the audience, like when the words of the song say,

In the middle of the program I skate to "Parlami d'amore, Mariu," I drop to my knees to express the emotion of the title, which means "Speak to Me of Love, Mariu."

66

"The stars in the sky" and the skater holds up a star and points to the sky.

I've found that it's hard working with choreographers who don't know ice skating, because they don't understand why skaters can't do certain moves on the ice or how much ice a skater has to cover. I worked with one guy who wanted to do a program with no crossovers. And I said, "Well, it's going to be hard for me to travel one hundred eighty-five feet with no crossovers."

Every time I hear music, I imagine myself skating to it. I'll be sitting in the audience at a Broadway show, listening to an actor sing an emotional song from a show like *Les Misérables*, or *Phantom of the Opera*, and I'll start thinking, "Hmm, what kind of move would I make to express that line? What kind of jump would I do during that crescendo?"

I once asked Janet Lynn, the five-time U.S. champion and 1972 Olympic bronze medalist, "Does that ever stop? Do you still imagine yourself skating to beautiful music that comes on?" And she said, "Yeah, I still do."

Skaters should choose the type of music that's best for them. For a competition, skaters usually use classical music because the judges like it. For me, it wouldn't be the best decision to pick a hard rock 'n' roll song for an important competition. I could do it, but a classical or epic piece would probably be better. I like music that's symphonic—big, classical, grand, and lyrical.

I also like to pick music that's unique or unexpected. Some music is used over and over in competitions. I have at least two thousand CDs in my own collection. When I'm choosing music for a new program, I listen to thousands of songs, thinking, "Could this be a long program? Could this be an artistic program?"

My problem is that I like a wide variety of music. I think, "I'd really like to do a classical piece." I'll start by listening to classical—then I'll hear a jazz piece that I really like and I think, "Well, maybe jazz. Well, maybe Big Band." Music choice is important because I'll listen and skate to the piece many times.

Before the invention of cassette tapes, skaters had to have their competition music cut and transferred to record albums. These records are from my early days as a competitive skater.

COSTUME RULES

The International Skating Union (ISU) and every amateur national skating organization has rules about what skaters should or should not wear on the ice. The overall rule is that costumes should be "modest, dignified, and appropriate for athletic competition."

For example, a woman's costume should cover her hips and posterior and should not expose her midriff. She should avoid one-piece outfits, such as a unitard, and any garish or theatrical costume. Men can't wear sleeveless shirts or tights.

Violations of these rules can result in a 0.1 or 0.2 deduction from a skater's score.

Unfortunately, bad taste can never be regulated out of existence.

Phillippe Candeloro of France received deductions at the 1992 World Championships because his costume lacked sleeves.

East Germany's Katarina Witt wore a featherless version of this costume at the 1988 European championships and was widely criticized. To be on the safe side, she added feathers around the hips for the 1988 Winter Olympics and skated to her second Olympic gold medal. Later the International Skating Union passed a rule that all ladies' dresses must have skirts.

COSTUME COSTS

Dorothy Hamill skated to an Olympic gold medal in 1976 wearing a pink stretch-knit dress sewn by a friend's mother; it cost $75. Nancy Kerrigan won her silver medal at the 1994 Olympics wearing a designer creation that boasted 11,500 rhinestones and that would have cost $13,000! (The designer donated it to Kerrigan.)

Dave Black

Costumes are another crucial part of a skater's presentation on the ice. When skaters start out, they usually don't have a lot of money for costumes, so many mothers sew costumes for their children. My mom didn't make my costumes but she shopped for material for my shirts and pants. After I won the Pacific Coast Junior Championships and was going to the National Championships, one of the judges pulled Linda aside and said, "He needs to change costumes before Nationals. They'll never let him win if he's wearing those ugly costumes." I was wearing a pumpkin-orange costume for my short, and a red, red, red costume for my long. I was a kid and I just chose the colors that I liked: orange and red.

For my first professional studio photograph, I wore my first skating costume created by a professional designer.

So my mom found someone in Los Angeles who made great skating costumes. We flew there twice before Nationals for fittings. I changed to a simple black costume for my long program and a rust costume with studs for my short program. I won the championship. I could have won wearing an ugly costume, but it certainly helped that I had a better look.

It's a good idea for skaters to practice in their costumes. Sometimes they don't and wish they had; they might split a seam in an embarrassing place or find out that they need more stretch in the material. Once I had sleeves that were so big that they covered my face when I did a triple Lutz and I couldn't see. You want to correct that kind of mistake before competition. A designer I work with in San Francisco watches videotapes of my practices to see what kind of moves I'm doing before she creates my costume.

My least-favorite costume ever was the military outfit that I wore in the 1988 U.S. Nationals, a month before the Olympics. It was constructed of heavy material and I could hardly stretch in it. So I had another one made of thinner, more elastic material for the Olympics—and it was seven pounds lighter, too!

Linda and I look over
costume sketches for my
1988 Olympic program.
I asked that the designer
make the sleeves smaller
on the short program
costume (left) and lower
the collar on the long
program costume (right).

GREAT COSTUMES

Skaters should wear costumes that complement their bodies, and avoid costumes that make the audience focus on the costume rather than the skater.

If you have a great figure, you can wear something simple that drapes and flows well in the breeze. I love the look of hair flying and material fluttering as a skater speeds across the ice.

Scott Hamilton started a return to the trend for male skaters to compete without sequins. He wanted audiences to see figure skating as a sport, so he wore an outfit that looked like a speed skater's suit for his gold-medal-winning performance at the 1984 Winter Olympics.

Today, many skaters, like Elvis Stojko, wear street clothes on the ice. Most clothes you buy in stores aren't made to raise your arms overhead or do splits, the way costumes are, so you have to look around and try different things on. But there's no better way to get a street look than to skate in regular clothes.

First woman to skate in short skirts: Sonja Henie, at the 1924 Winter Olympics. She was only eleven years old at the time. Older women were required to wear long skirts down to their ankles.

Scott Hamilton (top) demonstrates the no-frills look that many male skaters prefer today. Elvis Stojko (bottom) shows the street-wise look.

Costumes often help me communicate to the audience what kind of character I'm portraying. When I filmed Carmen on Ice, *my character was a soldier who had fallen from grace and was wearing rags. The costume was made of raw silk that was smudged with shoe polish to look old and dirty.*

Dave Black

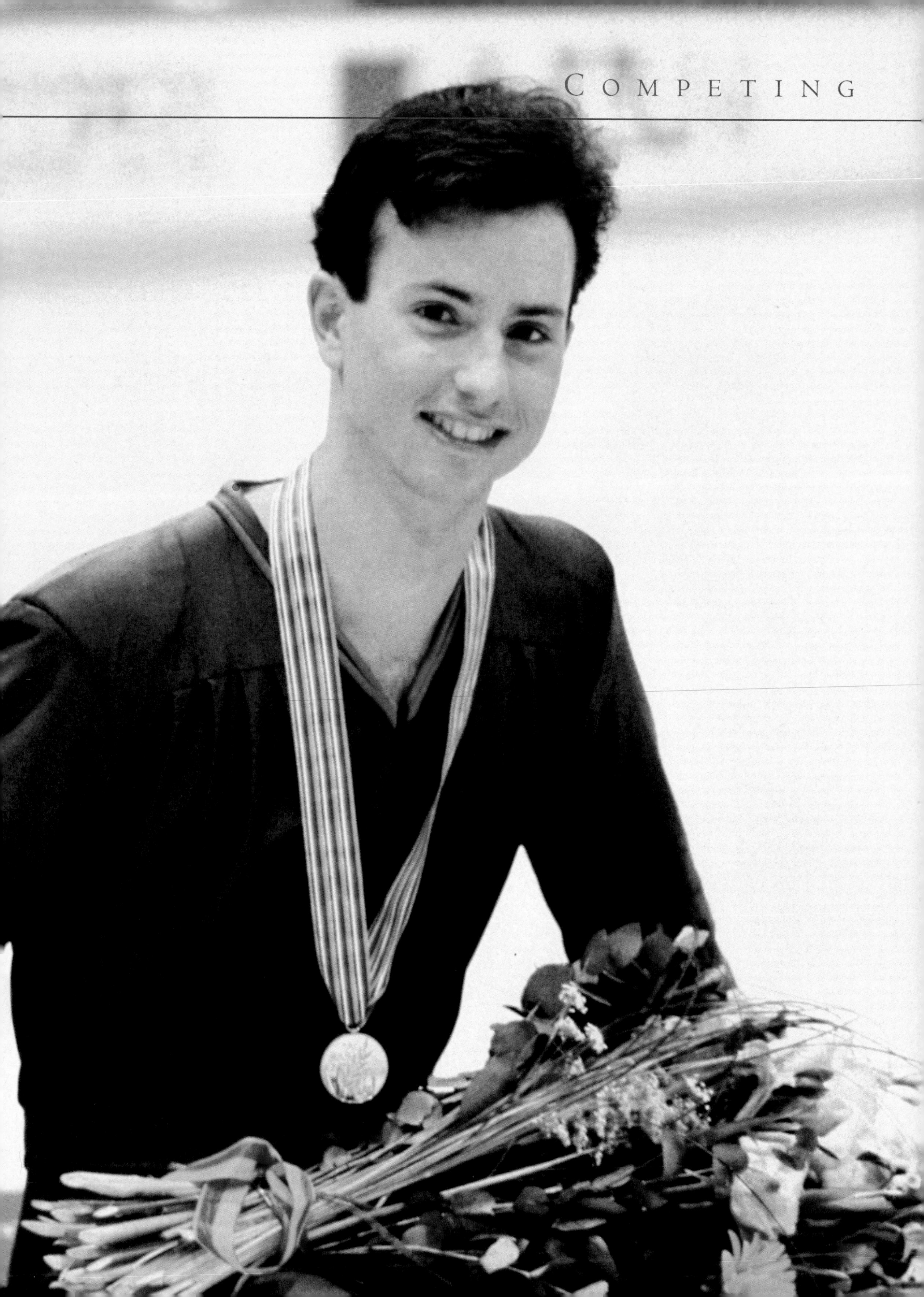

$\mathcal{I}$ WAS EIGHT AND A HALF YEARS OLD when I entered my first competition in the Pixie Derby Boys division. Before the competition started, I was waiting for Linda out in the parking lot with my skates already on.

When she drove up in her car, I went over and said, "Linda, how will I know when it's time to skate?"

She said, "A man who's a referee will come get you." But I was just as detail-oriented then as I am now; I needed to know *everything*. So I kept saying, "But how will I know it's my turn?" She kept repeating that the referee would tell me, that everything would be fine.

And, of course, it was. I competed with one other skater. We had to do three moves: a two-foot spin, crossovers both ways, and a mohawk (a simple skating turn that requires a change of feet). I spun my brains out, and I won. When I came off the ice, I told Linda that I didn't even breathe when I was out there—that's how excited I was.

Competitions were fun because Linda would bring all her students. We'd stay in hotel rooms, jump on the beds, ride the elevators, and eat out together. It was a blast.

Of course, every skater is nervous before a competition. You can't avoid that. But being nervous is different than being afraid. I felt nervous because I wanted to skate as well as I could. I wasn't afraid; to me, fear means that you don't trust yourself or your abilities. Fear makes you shut down. If you can control your nerves—if you realize that your nervousness is really about wanting to do a great job—then you can make them work for you.

Many people don't realize that the judges attend the practice sessions at competitions. They watch all the programs

First time figure skating was included in the Olympics:
1908 (Summer) Games in London, England. First Winter Olympics: 1924 in Chamonix, France.

Look out i

Here com

Brian Boitano vainqueur des

Boit

L'oppo

Boitano ic

Nine year old wins the gold

Brian Boitano, a fourth grader at St. Joseph of Cupertino school, won a gold medal in the preliminary men's 12 years and under ice skating competition held recently in Burlingame. Judging at the central California interclub competition was based on figures and free style. Brian took first in both.

This is the fourth medal for Brian, a 9-year-old member of the Sunnyvale Silver Edge figure skating club. He has been skating 14 months and has won two other gold medals and a silver medal.

ce world!

es Boitano

Mondiaux chez les hommes

eapfrogs

ne Boitano

Tekeekö Boitano ensimmäisenä neloshypyn?

es victory

COMPETITIVE HISTORY

1972	1st Place, Pixie Derby Boys, Central California Interstate Association (CCIA)
1972	Preliminary Test
1972	1st Place, Preliminary Boys, Seattle, Washington
1972	2nd Place, Preliminary Boys, Ontario, California
1973	1st Place, Preliminary Boys, CCIA
1973	1st Test
1973	1st Place, First Test Boys, Squaw Valley, California
1973	2nd Place, First Test Boys, Seattle, Washington
1973	2nd Place, First Test Boys, Central Pacific
1974	1st Place, First Test Boys, Golden West
1974	2nd Test
1974	1st Place, Juvenile Boys Central Pacific Regional Championship
1974	1st Place, Juvenile Boys Pacific Coast Sectional Championships
1975	3rd Test
1975	1st Place, Intermediate Men Central Pacific Regional Championships
1975	1st Place, Intermediate Men Pacific Coast Sectional Championships
1976	4th Test
1976	5th Test
1976	1st Place, Novice Men Junior Olympics
1976	1st Place, Novice Men Central Pacific Regional Championships
1976	1st Place, Novice Men Pacific Coast Sectional Championships
1977	3rd Place, Novice Men National Championships; 1st Place, Freestyle
1977	6th Test
1977	7th Test
1977	1st Place, Junior Men Sun Valley Championships
1977	1st Place, Junior Men Central Pacific Regional Championships
1977	1st Place, Junior Men Pacific Coast Sectional Championships
1978	1st Place, Junior Men National Championships
1978	3rd Place, Junior Men World Championships
1978	8th Test
1978	1st Place, Senior Men Vienna International Championships
1978	8th Place, U.S. Sports Festival
1979	3rd Place, Senior Men Pacific Coast Sectional Championships
1979	8th Place, Senior Men National Championships
1979	3rd Place, Grand Prix St. Gervais International
1979	3rd Place, Nebelhorn Trophy
1979	5th Place, U.S. Sports Festival
1980	5th Place, Skate Canada; Brian Boitano lands the first 'Tano triple Lutz in competition
1980	2nd Place, Senior Men Pacific Coast Sectional Championships
1980	5th Place, Senior Men National Championships
1980	Alternate for U.S. Olympic team
1981	1st Place, Senior Men Pacific Coast Sectional Championships
1981	4th Place, Senior Men National Championships
1981	3rd Place, U.S. Sports Festival
1981	3rd Place, Skate America
1982	1st Place, Senior Men Pacific Coast Sectional Championships
1982	4th Place, Senior Men National Championships; Brian Boitano becomes the first American to land a triple Axel in national competition
1982	1st Place, U.S. Sports Festival
1982	1st Place, Ennia Cup
1982	1st Place, Skate Canada
1983	1st Place, Senior Men Pacific Coast Sectional Championships
1983	2nd Place, Senior Men National Championships
1983	7th Place, World Championships; Brian Boitano becomes the first skater to land all 6 triple jumps in a World competition
1983	1st Place, Skate America
1984	1st Place, Senior Men Pacific Coast Sectional Championships
1984	2nd Place, Senior Men National Championships
1984	5th Place, Olympic Winter Games
1984	6th Place, World Championships
1984	1st Place, St. Ivel International
1984	3rd Place, NHK Trophy
1985	1st Place, Senior Men National Championships
1985	3rd Place, World Championships
1985	1st Place, U.S. Sports Festival
1985	2nd Place, Skate America
1985	1st Place, NHK Trophy
1986	1st Place, Senior Men National Championships

1986	1st Place, World Championships	1994	1st Place, World Professional Championships
1986	1st Place, U.S. Olympic Festival	1995	1st Place, Gold Championship
1986	1st Place, Skate America	1995	1st Place, Ice Wars, U.S.A. team member
1987	1st Place, Senior Men National Championships	1995	1st Place, Skate x 2
1987	2nd Place, World Championships	1995	1st Place, Men's Outdoor Professional Championship
1987	2nd Place, Skate Canada	1995	2nd Place, World Professional Championships
1987	1st Place, Novarat Trophy	1996	1st Place, Gold Championship
1988	1st Place, Senior Men National Championships	1996	1st Place, Ice Wars, U.S.A. team member
1988	1st Place, Olympic Winter Games	1996	1st Place, Battle of the Sexes
1988	1st Place, World Championships	1996	2nd Place, Men's Professional Championships
1988	1st Place, World Professional Championships	1996	2nd Place, World Professional Championships
1988	1st Place, Challenge of Champions		
1989	1st Place, World Professional Championships		
1989	1st Place, Challenge of Champions		
1990	1st Place, World Professional Championships		
1990	1st Place, Challenge of Champions		
1991	1st Place, World Professional Championships		
1991	1st Place, Challenge of Champions		
1991	1st Place, Les Dieux de la Glace, Paris, France		
1992	1st Place, World Professional Championships		
1992	3rd Place, Challenge of Champions		
1993	1st Place, Fall Pro-Am Challenge		
1994	1st Place, Spring Pro-Am Challenge		
1994	2nd Place, National Championships		
1994	6th Place, Olympic Winter Games		
1994	2nd Place, Gold Championship		
1994	1st Place, Ice Wars, U.S.A. team member		
1994	1st Place, Men's Outdoor Professional Championship		
1994	1st Place, Nikon Championship		

SILVER EDGE
FSC

Group A

2nd Place

Tuck Loop

August 16, 1974

SILVER EDGE
FSC

Group A

3rd Place

Double Toe
Bally

August 9, 1974

SILVER EDGE
FSC

Group A

2nd Place

Split Jump
Double Toe
Loop

August 23, 1974

U.S.A

USFSA

Presented By

THE UNITED STATES
FIGURE SKATING ASSOCIATION

To

Brian Boitano

In Recognition of Competitive Participation in The

Novice Men's Event

UNITED STATES
FIGURE SKATING CHAMPIONSHIPS

Held at *Hartford, Connecticut* On *February 2–5, 1977*

WHY SKATERS
GET EXHAUSTED

Even though the men's long program only lasts four and a half minutes, and the ladies' long program for four minutes, skaters are usually exhausted by the finish. I spend ten to twelve months working on a competitive program and building up stamina. Still, it's always hard, mainly because skating combines aerobic and anaerobic activity.

In fact, skating a long program is like running a race that is part sprint and part marathon. A sprinter runs a race in fifteen seconds, so he expends all his energy in one short and intense burst. That's the kind of energy a skater puts forth to do a triple jump.

But after that triple jump, the skater keeps going. He does footwork sequences and spins. That part of the program requires stamina, which is similar to a long-distance race. Then he has to gather himself together to launch another triple—with another burst of energy—then go back to the long-distance race again! I've never found another sport or exercise that duplicates the amount of energy and the shifts of energy that I need in skating.

they expect to judge before the actual event. The judges aren't supposed to talk among themselves or compare notes; most of the time, they sit in the stands and concentrate on watching each skater's program. During the competition, they must place as many as thirty skaters in the correct order and they only have about four or five minutes to assess each performance. It's a tough job. I think it helps the judges to observe practices and become familiar with the skaters' abilities and programs.

As you might expect, skaters do think about impressing the judges when they're practicing at a competition. The better a skater performs in practice, the more likely that the judges will think that skater is capable of winning. When you hear people talk about which skater is "winning" the practice sessions it means the judges have noticed which skater is skating the best during practice and may mentally place that skater a little higher than the others.

More important than winning practice sessions, however, is getting prepared and feeling ready for the competition. If I was having trouble with a jump, I'd focus on doing just one good one. Also, I paced myself in the practice sessions to conserve energy for the competition. If I was skating with an injury, instead of jumping, I spent my time on the preparation and entry, then visualized the jump itself. I knew that, if my entry was solid, my jump would be good. To keep up my confidence, I always tried to finish a practice with a well-executed move.

Some competitors watch the other skaters practice. I never did that. I left the rink to concentrate on my own preparation. While I rested, Linda watched my competitors and passed on anything that might give me an edge.

The night before a competition, I usually ate pasta for dinner. I typically ate with Linda, rather than other skaters, because I was already trying to focus. I tried as hard as I could to avoid thinking about the next day, because nervousness uses up so much energy. I rarely talked to Linda about what I was feeling because there didn't seem much point. After all, I'd only say, "I feel nervous."

No kidding.

At most competitions, skaters stay in a hotel. But at the 1988 Olympics, the eight U. S. male skaters shared a four-bedroom apartment—with one bathroom. Most of the time, everybody knew they had to be quiet because it was

THE ETIQUETTE OF PRACTICE SESSIONS

Nancy Kerrigan and Tonya Harding had to skate in the same practice session in the 1994 Winter Olympics, despite the fact that Tonya's bodyguard was involved in the attack on Nancy at the U.S. National Championships.

If you're sitting in the audience and watching six skaters zoom around the rink during a practice session, you may wonder why they don't crash into each other more often. Skaters learn basic rules to follow during a practice that help keep order. In my opinion, skaters make really good drivers because years of skating practice sessions have taught them how to figure out who has the right of way.

The first rule is that the skater whose music is playing has the right of way; everyone else skates around him.

The second rule is that the skater who starts setting up for a jump first always gets the right of way. In other words, if I'm just stroking around the ice and I see Todd Eldredge doing back crossovers to set up for a jump, I stay out of his way.

Skaters will make eye contact as they're approaching each other to indicate whether they're going to pass on the right or the left. I always lean my head in the direction that I plan to go. Other skaters will point—although sometimes that gets confusing, because a skater will point to the left and it will make me think, "Does that mean *I'm* supposed to go left or *he's* going left?"

Most of the time, this system works well, but it's not foolproof. In 1986, I ran into Nancy Kerrigan when we were skating in a crowded session. I was going into a jump, so I had a lot of momentum, and all 170 pounds of me hit 110 pounds of her. She went flying. I couldn't even move; I just stood there while people picked her up. She had to go to the hospital and get stitches in her elbow. I was so relieved when I found out she would be okay. Now we laugh about that on tour. Sometimes I jokingly say, "Watch out or I'll get the other elbow!"

During a competition practice, some skaters will try to throw off your concentration or distract you by coming right up behind you. That's just a mind game they play, hoping to psych you out.

such an important competition. But one of the ice dancers insisted on watching the opening ceremonies on the apartment's TV, even though one of the pair skaters wanted to turn the TV off. He and his partner were skating the next day and the TV announcers were discussing their chances of winning a medal. He didn't want to hear it.

I don't blame him. A couple of times during that Olympics, I bought a newspaper and saw an article on "The Battle of the Brians" on the front page. I always threw the paper away. I didn't want to know what was being written or said about me.

On the day of the competition, I would start to focus at the hotel, before I went to the rink. I meditated and focused on breathing deeply from my solar plexus. During my meditation, I'd imagine that I was surrounded by a protective bubble and that everybody's negative energy was bouncing off of it.

That focus helped me when competitors tried to psych me out. For example, one skater at the 1988 Olympics had a habit of trying to unnerve me. The night of the short program, I arrived at the arena a little later than usual, but still in plenty of time. He saw me and said, "Hurry up and get your skates on! Everyone's going on the ice for warm-up!" I panicked for a second, until I realized that he was just trying to shake my confidence. That's the kind of negativity I tried to ward off by creating the bubble.

About a year after the 1988 Winter Olympics I performed with Brian Orser at Sun Valley, Idaho (left). I think the audience liked to see that despite our Olympic rivalry, we were good friends who could laugh and have fun together.

(Opposite page) Paul Wylie (center) and Christopher Bowman (right) were my U.S. teammates at the 1988 Winter Olympics. I can't imagine teammates being any closer. Ten years later, Paul and I were both in Chris's wedding.

INTERNATIONAL FRIENDSHIPS

All skaters want to win, so they're fiercely competitive on the ice. I think it should be a different story off the ice. I never wished for anything bad to happen to my competitors—in fact, I always wanted to be friends with them.

When I was competing, there was still a major division between the East and the West. Still, I always tried to talk to the Russian skaters, because I didn't think politics should stand in the way of sports or friendships. At first, they were a little afraid to talk to me. I'd hear later that people told them that they shouldn't hang out too much with Americans. Although many of the Russians understood English, they often pretended that they didn't to keep other skaters from trying to communicate with them.

I really wanted to be friends with Alexandr Fadeev, whom everyone called Sasha. I thought he was a great skater; he totally

dominated in 1985 and was one of my archrivals in 1988. I could tell he liked me, but he wouldn't talk to me at first. But I just kept trying and we ended up being really good friends.

At competitions, Alexeyvich Zhuk, one of the Russian coaches, used to comb the halls at night to make sure that all the Russian skaters were in their rooms. I used to help Sasha sneak out of his room to have fun with the other skaters.

In 1986, I went to Russia for the Goodwill Games and Sasha took me to the Kremlin. He gave me his army hat, with the hammer and sickle on the front, and a religious icon for my mother. When he and his wife had a baby, I gave him a St. Anthony medal and he said, "I hope my son turns out like you." In the end, those kinds of friendships mean as much as winning medals.

SKATING HURT

Sometimes I skated in a competition even though I was sick or injured, because the event was too important to miss. I always checked with my doctor first. When I was 14, I got the flu at the World Junior Championships and kept throwing up. I couldn't take any medicine or I would have violated drug regulations, so Linda and I went to a doctor and got something to calm my stomach. We didn't tell anyone that I was sick because we didn't want judges to think I was skating in a weakened condition. Somehow I managed to make it through my program and I won the bronze medal.

I've skated with stress fractures, repetitive stress injuries, and tendonitis. The only injury that kept me off the ice for a long period of time occurred when I was twelve and trying to learn the triple Salchow. My knee hurt, so my parents took me to our doctor. We found out that I had jumper's knee: the tendons were so overdeveloped for my muscle structure that my kneecap had cracked all over. I couldn't skate at all for six months, then for three months I could only practice figures. The silver lining was that I became very proficient at figures, and began to really enjoy practicing them.

The reality is that skaters don't get to the elite level if they let a little flu or fever stop them—although it's *very* important to talk to your parents, coach, and doctor and make sure that everyone agrees that you should skate. In fact, in one international competition, I won the gold medal skating with a heel injury, the silver medalist was recovering from pneumonia, and the bronze medalist was suffering a knee problem. None of us let pain keep us from competing.

Once I was at the rink, I liked to face the pressure of competition right away, so I'd take a look at the crowd as soon as I arrived. Other skaters may put on a Walkman and listen to music to block out distractions. But as competition time got closer, I'd make the bubble more solid and focused. I used to feel that if I saw someone I knew backstage and didn't smile or say hello, that person would get mad at me. But every time you say hello, you use up a little bit of energy, so I always looked down so that I wouldn't catch anyone's eye. I wouldn't pay attention to anything outside of the bubble and I wouldn't hear anything that I didn't want to hear. The only other person allowed in that bubble was Linda. We usually didn't talk, but we connected with our eyes. I could go the whole night without saying a word.

I'm not unique in my focus. The atmosphere is really thick backstage before a competition; most skaters keep to themselves and usually don't talk much. Scott Hamilton was an exception to the rule. Scott could socialize and talk to people backstage, then he'd step on the ice, his music would start and he'd be totally focused on his program. I usually stayed out of the dressing room as much as possible before I skated, because sometimes skaters in there who had already finished with their programs talked about how they or one of their competitors had skated. I didn't want to hear about that.

During the 1982 Skate Canada competition, I was waiting in the dressing room with Brian Orser when another skater came in after competing. He wanted Orser to win, so he tried to psych me out by telling Brian Orser that the ice was perfect for him, that Orser could probably do a triple-triple combination in place of another jump he had planned, and so on.

After that, I made it a point to hang out with skaters who hadn't competed yet, because they were thinking about what they needed to do; they didn't have energy for anything else.

After I put on my costume, I started getting even more focused. It was always in the back of my mind that in half an hour I'd be on the ice.

As I'm waiting to skate, I definitely experience ups and downs. I'll start to get nervous, then I'll calm myself down. Then I'll get tense again, and I'll calm myself again.

(Opposite page) I usually stretch for about half an hour before a practice session at a competition.

That cycle keeps repeating, which is why waiting is so exhausting, and why it's so important to occupy my mind in the right way.

During the six-minute warm-up, I would focus on each jump and move I had planned. After the warm-up, the waiting would begin. That was the real killer. Some skaters preferred some recovery time after the warm-up, but I liked to skate first. The longer the wait, the more nervous I got. Plus, my muscles would still be warm at that point. Skating first isn't the best position for scores, because the judges have to leave some high marks in case another skater does a better job. But I was more interested in skating well.

If I drew the last position, the wait could be more than a half-hour. If I had a long wait, I always took off my skates, so that my feet wouldn't fall asleep. Then I'd run or jump—anything to keep a light sweat. If you stop sweating, you get chilled and it's extremely difficult to skate well.

At the 1987 World Championships, for example, I did one of the best quads of my life during the warm-up. Then I had to wait for more than thirty minutes to skate. I must have cooled off a little too much or got a little too tired, because when I finally skated my program, I turned out of the quad. When you're waiting, you have to walk

KEEPING WARM

To keep warm in a cold rink:

♦ Always wear layers; if you get warmer or colder, you can easily adjust what you're wearing.

♦ Keep your skates in a warm place. If they get cold at the rink, blow some hot air inside the boot with a hair dryer.

♦ Stretch your muscles before stepping onto the ice; it's better for your muscles and helps prevent injuries.

♦ Coaches and parents can wear warmers in their gloves. Skaters can wear them when they're working on figures.

After stepping on the ice to skate my long program at the 1988 Winter Olympics, I perform a ritual that always makes my mom really nervous: retying my boot laces one more time.

86

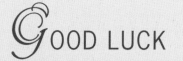

GOOD LUCK

Competitions are so nerve-racking that many skaters develop superstitious rituals or carry good-luck charms, hoping to give themselves an extra edge. Even if it's all in the mind, sometimes it's comforting to feel you have something extra in your corner.

When I was competing, I'd always put my left skate on first. That actually developed for a practical reason: because I land on my right foot, that boot would need the most adjustment, so I left it for last.

I also used to carry a bent nail from the stage at the San Francisco opera in my skating bag; that was supposed to bring good luck.

Katarina Witt had three stuffed animals that friends gave her that she felt brought her good luck. One was an angel and the other two were fantasy animals. She always carried them around in her skating bag. When she was skating in a competition, a friend held them for her.

Elizabeth Punsalen, who skates with her ice dancing partner Jerod Swallow, always ties her right skate first before a competition. She started that ritual after hearing that Kristi Yamaguchi did it on her way to winning the Olympic gold medal.

Michelle Kwan used to have a lot of superstitions—if she stepped on the ice with her left skate and performed well, for example, she'd try to do that all the time—but she gave them up because she felt she was focusing too much on the superstitions and not enough on skating. However, both Michelle and her sister Karen, who's also a competitive skater, wear gold Chinese dragon charms on necklaces for good luck.

Oksana Baiul always steps onto the ice with her left skate, and Elvis Stojko always wears a necklace during competition. His mom gave him the necklace, and his aunt and uncle gave him the charm that hangs on it. The charm is a round medallion with the logo for the sixteenth Winter Olympic Games on one side and the slogan, "Elvis, You're Number One!" on the other side.

a fine line between running around to keep warm and trying to conserve your energy without cooling off.

I never watched other skaters compete as I waited. That was a little superstition on my part. I didn't perform well the one time that I watched somebody during a competition, so I decided I'd never do it again. Plus, it's more nerve-racking for me to watch someone else than to sit by myself in the dressing room.

Before I stepped on the ice, I always tried to find a moment when I could be absolutely peaceful. I'd relax my shoulders and arms, and watch my breath go up and down in my abdomen. I wasn't thinking, "I've got to take my skate guards off." I wasn't thinking, "I've got to get on my costume." I think trees are like that; they don't worry or fret, they just . . . sit there. I'd try to hold that feeling of being a tree for about fifteen seconds.

The most intense moment during competitions was when the skater before me was one minute from the end of his program. That's when I'd tighten my laces for the last time. (To prevent a lace from breaking at that crucial point, I always changed my laces a week before the competition.)

I didn't feel fear at that point, but I felt an incredibly heightened sense of tension. Months and months of training and hard work had built up to *that very moment* and I wanted to do a great job.

Then the announcer would call my name. I'd skate out on the ice and take my starting position. At that point, I wasn't aware of the audience; I deliberately blocked out the sights and sounds of the crowd. I wanted to concentrate completely on my skating and have what I call "energy to the moment."

My music would start and the tension would vanish. Then all I had to do was skate.

DON'T LISTEN TO MURPHY

Once I was backstage at a competition, waiting to skate, and I could hear the audience going wild over a fabulous performance by Scott Hamilton. As I waited and listened to the crowd, all I did was worry about what would happen if I missed my triple Lutz. That little negative voice in my head kept repeating, "What if I miss the Lutz? What if I miss the Lutz?" (I call that voice "Murphy," after Murphy's Law, which says that whatever can go wrong, will go wrong.)

Finally, it was my turn. I went out on the ice and, sure enough, I missed the Lutz. After that, I told myself, "I'll never again say, 'what if, what if?' I'm always going to fill my mind with the one thought that will make the jump good."

So when I hear "Murphy" talking in my head, I deliberately change each negative statement into a positive one. Instead of thinking, "If I don't get the right arm back, then I won't land the jump," I think, "Get your right arm back and you *will* land the jump." It helps a lot.

I've heard coaches tell their skaters, "Don't think. Go out there and just do it." But I need to think of *something* to block out all the pressure, because thoughts will fill your head no matter what. And guess what? Nine times out of ten, they'll be negative thoughts. So I fill my mind by talking to myself about what I need to do technically.

For example, at the beginning of my Olympic program, I breathed in when the music started, then I turned my head, then I started talking to myself, "Stretch and turn, one, two, three, mohawk, back, drop, back, arm . . ." and so on. I'll even count my crossovers as I do them. I talk to myself all the time.

It keeps me from listening to Murphy.

LINDA LEAVER ON PREPARATION

Compulsory figures are skated with a slow glide. A skater shouldn't go too slowly, or his blade will wobble on the ice, which results in a deduction. As the skater nears the top or the middle of the figure eight, he pushes off again with one skate to give additional momentum. Although figures are no longer required for freestyle competitions, some skaters still compete in figures-only contests.

Preparation is the key to confidence and winning. The best example of that was the 1987 Skate Canada competition. It was held in Calgary, the site for the 1988 Winter Olympics. The Canadians wanted to showcase their team, so they asked the USFSA to send B-level skaters. They didn't want Brian Boitano to skate.

But I wanted Brian there so he could get used to the ice rinks where the Olympic competitions would be held. I went to the USFSA committee meeting where it would be decided which skaters would compete in which international event, and I spoke for twenty minutes on why Brian should be there. I said that the Canadians' request was unreasonable and detrimental to the American team's best interests.

My appearance was a big deal; coaches *never* went to those meetings. But skaters don't get many practices at the Olympics; sometimes they don't even have any practice in the rink where the competition is held. Familiarity with the rinks and ice surfaces is vital. The committee voted and the vote was pretty close, but Brian was allowed to compete.

The Calgary site had three

different rinks, one each for figures, the short program, and the long program. At Skate Canada, Brian became familiar with each venue, including their ice texture, surface size, lighting, and overall feel. It was an invaluable experience for him.

As it turned out, Brian skated two of his finest performances ever at Skate Canada, but came in second. I didn't really care because I was so happy with the way he skated. Brian's placement was controversial and the judges started talking about how good he was, how much his programs had improved, how high he could jump.

After Skate Canada, he had four months until the Olympics and he trained even harder. He made hundreds of changes in that time, everything from spin position, to the direction his footwork was facing, to what section of ice he would choose for his figures. He even changed the color of his short program costume, because it looked washed-out in the competition rink.

When Brian went to the Olympics, he had two sets of blades, a backup costume for each event, backup music tapes—he had backups for everything. It was such an important competition; Brian didn't want to worry about missing costumes, broken blades, or lost tapes.

He never let his skates out of his sight at the competition. They were either under his arm or with his parents or me. Over the years, we had seen all kinds of things happen. At one competition, a skater's blades were stolen; at another, a skater's blades were vandalized. So Brian always took precautions.

Every practice at a competition offers another chance to prepare and to focus on what you need to do to ensure your best performance. Some skaters spend too much energy competing in the practice sessions and not enough focusing on their preparation. (It amazes me how many skaters know that they have to do a four-and-a-half-minute program with spins, footwork, and eight triples without stopping—and never practice that.)

After the figures at the 1988 Olympics, Brian was in second place, ahead of Brian Orser. The next event was the short, or technical, program. Brian had a defensive strategy for the short: skate clean, make no errors, and leave some energy for the long program.

Brian was second in the short, second in figures, and first overall by a narrow margin. He had skated fabulously, with no errors, but he was a little hungry going into the long program because he hadn't won the short. I think he felt he had more in him and he wanted to show it.

He turned what could have been a negative—coming in second—into a positive. Brian skated on the last night feeling that he was in the perfect position.

It was a close, hard-fought competition, and it took Brian's ultimate performance to win. That's what made it so wonderful. When you win, you want to know that you tested yourself against the other skaters' best.

JOAN GRUBER ON JUDGING

Joan Gruber is an ISU championship judge who has logged forty years judging figure skating competitions. Here's what she has to say about judging, one of the most misunderstood aspects of figure skating:

Dave Black

I grew up in the Philadelphia area and skated at the national level. I trained in the summers at a huge center in Lake Placid that held skating tests every Sunday. One day when I was sixteen years old, I went to the rink because some of my friends were taking tests. A group of us asked for clipboards and were allowed to go on the ice and try to "trial" judge. I had never had the experience of being a judge. It turned out to be challenging and a lot of fun.

I continued to trial judge. That's where you go to competitions and judge skaters, then have a monitor look at your result to see how well you agreed with the official judging panel. Once you've shown enough expertise at trial judging, you can become a judge, too. I became a judge when I was eighteen. Judging offers a way for people who love the sport to stay involved even if they aren't committed enough or talented enough to keep competing.

There are judges for skating tests and for competitions. On the competition side, you progress through novice, junior, senior, national, and international levels. The highest level is a championship (world) judge who is eligible to judge the Olympics and World Championships. Most people specialize in one or two events. I judge singles and pair competitions.

The biggest misconception about figure skating judges is how much education and expertise we have.

I'm sure the public thinks we're just people pulled in off the street to judge, especially when they don't agree with how we scored their favorite skater.

But every four years, judges are required to go to judging schools; some last one day, some last for a weekend. Depending on the level of judging you're learning, you'll be shown different things. Sometimes skating clubs will do demonstrations, where you learn to recognize jumps and spins. Or the skaters will all do a jump and we'll have to rate them from best to worst. Sometimes we'll watch competition videos. We'll learn about whatever is an issue at the moment. For example, if a new rule makes a certain pair lift illegal, we'll go over that. Once you're at the international level, you also have to attend international schools once every four years.

Judges attend the practice sessions that are held before a competition, not so we can pre-judge the competition, as some people think; it just helps judges sort out the general ability level for each skater. For example, say you're watching ten skaters during practice. Nine are doing triple-triple jump combinations, one is doing a double-double combination. There's no way that skater will beat the others, so in your mind, you're thinking he's about a 4.5. But maybe he just wasn't skating up to par the day you saw him practice and he hits his triple-triple combination in the competition. Then he may move up to a 5.5 in your mind. On the other hand, you may see a skater hit all his triples in practice, then he mops up the ice during the competition. His marks automatically go down.

As we're judging a competition, we have sheets to keep track of what we see. Everybody has his own system, but it has to be pretty organized. You check off the jumps and spins as the skater does them. I count the number of rotations in a spin, so that if two skaters both did the same spin, I have a note about which one did more revolutions. I'll note other things, too, like which skater did footwork with a lot of changes of direction and which skater just did a spiral. Sometimes it's distracting to have to write everything down, because you can't really be a participant in the event. But when it's all over, you have great notes in case someone wants to know why you judged a skater the way you did.

After every international competition, the referee in charge reviews the judges' performance by going over every mark from every judge for every skater. You have to be ready to explain your marks if the referee questions them. The referee may say, "I don't agree with your placement of this skater because the music wasn't appropriate for the footwork." Then I may say, "But I felt the spin speed more than made up for that fifteen-second footwork sequence."

You go back and forth and the referee either agrees with you or makes you write a letter of explanation. You could get cautioned or put on a watch list or even suspended, if your marks are often in question. It's tough, because you want to be in line with the other judges' marks, but not to the point that you're not judging what you see on the ice.

I've often been booed by the audience when I give what they see as a low score. What they may not understand is that you have to compare all the scores a judge gives to see where he or she is placing the skaters.

For example, if I know I have to judge thirty-three skaters in an afternoon and the first skater is Todd Eldredge, I can't give him a 5.9/5.9, because I'd have almost nothing higher to give if the skaters that follow him do better. So I might give him a 5.7/5.8, just in case someone else skates and is dynamite. But if none of the remaining skaters is better, I have to keep giving lower and lower scores. I might give one skater a 4.9/5.0 while another judge gives him a 5.4/5.5—but we actually both ranked the skater in fifth place. When it's all over, I might have ranked all thirty-three skaters exactly the way the other judges did, and been booed thirty times.

One of the toughest things about being a judge is that you want to be fair and do the best job you can. You hope that you see everything that happens on the ice, although judges have been known to miss something when they glance down to make a note. Of course, we don't get to see slow-motion instant replays! You just have to make sure you're focused every moment.

Joan Gruber takes detailed notes on her score sheet as she judges a competition so she can keep track of how each skater performed.

HOW TO JUDGE A PROGRAM

Dave Black

It's often hard to judge a skater's program when you're watching it on TV. The camera angles change constantly, so you can't see the pattern of the whole program, and it's difficult to see how high the skater jumps. However, here's a quick guide to what judges look for, most of which you can see, even on television.

◆ Watch the speed and width of the skater's stride as he does his crossovers. Good crossovers are smooth; bad crossovers are jerky and uneven. Jill Trenary and Caryn Kadavy are examples of skaters with wonderful crossovers.

◆ Skaters should center their spins and stay in one spot. Watch the blade on the ice. There should be a little pile of snow or ice where the skater is spinning. If the skater moves sideways away from that pile it's called "traveling." A poor spin may travel five or more feet.

◆ Spins should be fast. Also note the quality of positions in spins. For example, the foot should be even with or higher than the head in a camel spin and the back should be arched. A sit spin should be low and a layback spin should be well arched. Different arm positions make the spin more difficult. Todd Eldredge has exceptionally fast spins, and Rudy Galindo has great positions.

◆ Watch footwork for intricacy and variety. Footwork immediately preceding a jump makes the jump more difficult. Scott Hamilton is renowned for his fast and light footwork.

◆ Once you're able to recognize the different jumps, watch closely to make sure that the takeoffs are from the correct edge. A common error is taking off on the inside edge rather than the outside edge for a Lutz jump,

Jill Trenary (right) exhibits beautiful, wide crossovers, while Todd Eldredge (below) spins so fast he seems to blur.

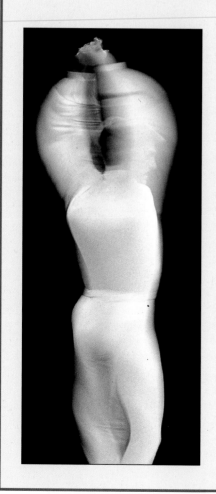

which turns the jump into a flip. A flip is easier than a Lutz, so it should get less credit.

◆ It's easy to see if a skater falls on a jump. But it's more difficult to determine differences in the quality of jumps. Watch for height, speed, position in the air, and control on the landing. A jump should be landed with speed and flow. The jump should be a seamless and integral part of the overall program. If a skater lands too far forward on his skate so that the toe picks hit the ice, it causes a scratchy landing. If a skater is leaning too far back on his landing, it can cause a loss of balance and a subsequent turn out of the jump. If I were judging a skater, I'd give him credit for trying a more difficult jump, even if he didn't land perfectly. Some judges, however, would rather see a less difficult program skated cleanly. That's why there will always be differences of opinion about marks!

◆ Notice the skater's landing position after a jump. The free leg should be held high, with a pointed toe, the head should be held erect, and the arms should be fully extended. Ilia Kulik and Michelle Kwan display beautiful landing positions.

◆ Watch the skater's air position. The ankles should be crossed. Midori Ito jumps with her ankle crossed at her calf; that's called a wrap and is not considered aesthetically pleasing. Jump height is also important; Alexi Urmanov and Ilia Kulik get incredible height on their jumps.

♦ When you're watching skating on TV, it's difficult to determine if the choreography is well balanced. However, there are some things to look for. The movement should face all four sides of the rink, and the program should also cover the entire ice surface. In a really well-rounded program, you'll see skaters doing crossovers in all four different directions—left forward, right forward, right back, and left back. Take particular note of Michelle Kwan's programs; they're models of balance and elegance.

♦ In many ways, artistic judgments are the hardest ones to make. Style preference is a matter of opinion. One person may prefer rock 'n' roll and another person may prefer classical music. So you have to say, "Okay, what music is best for this skater? What style is best? And how well is the skater's vision fulfilled?"

♦ It's important to be a real fighter in competition. That's Elvis Stojko's strength; he's a real warrior on the ice.

Ilia Kulik (top) gets incredible height on his jumps, as does Michelle Kwan (middle). Although Midori Ito jumped better than any other female skater of her time, judges didn't consider her crossed-leg position aesthetically pleasing (bottom).

JUDGES' COMMENTS

Some skaters can let criticism bounce off them, but that's difficult for me. Fortunately, Linda always knew that, so she filtered the comments she heard from the judges about my skating and just told me the constructive criticism.

In 1987, for example, one judge told her that I should quit skating because I was having too much trouble with my jumps—and another judge told Linda that she was holding me back from realizing my potential. Linda wisely chose not to pass either of those comments on to me—or to take them seriously herself.

Sometimes after a competition, Linda would ask the judges what we should do to make my program better. We listened to them, even if we disagreed, and Linda kept notebooks full of their advice.

Of course, different judges have different viewpoints. Some judges want your program to be more "edgy." Other judges may want more fast footwork, so you have to weigh the advice and consider the skater and the situation.

Over the years, I've had to develop a sense of humor about the criticism I've received. I've had judges criticize everything. One year, after doing four competitions, a judge came up to me and said, "I hated your hair at Skate America; at Skate Canada I thought it was okay; and it was the worst at the last competition. But now I like it."

Another time I skated in a blue and yellow costume at Skate America. An Italian judge said, "You have to get rid of that costume; you look like Superman out there."

When I was twelve or thirteen years old, a judge gave me low marks and criticized my skating because she said that I didn't land my jumps on the "booms" in the music. Linda pointed out to her that I was the only skater landing triples and the only one who didn't fall. Still, the judge insisted I deserved low marks for not landing my jumps on the booms.

It's tough to get so much criticism at a young age. The positive aspect is that I learned to be more empathetic toward other people and to listen to advice while still following my own instincts. I learned to listen to the criticism and pretend that it was being said about another skater, not about me. That helped me to really hear the comments, rather than denying them just because they hurt. Then I had to decide whether the criticism was valuable. I'd go to someone I trusted, usually Linda, and ask for another opinion. Then I could sift through all the advice and make my own decision about what to do.

(Opposite page) At competitions, volunteers pick up the bouquets of flowers that are tossed on the ice. They also have to pick up every loose petal, since even a single petal could make the next skaters trip and fall during their programs.

Highest scores for single performance: Jayne Torvill and Christopher Dean (Great Britain) received nine perfect 6.0's for artistic impression in their free dance at the 1984 Winter Olympics.

KNOW THE SCORE

The majority of ordinals (placements) by the judging panel wins the event, but the placements are factored into points for each event and added together. Here's how it works:

Short Program

Judge	1	2	3	4	5
Skater A	5.6	5.7	5.1	5.6	5.5
Skater B	5.5	5.8	5.2	5.4	5.3

Placements

Skater A	1	2	2	1	1
Skater B	2	1	1	2	2

Long Program

Judge	1	2	3	4	5
Skater A	4.9	5.0	5.2	5.1	4.8
Skater B	5.1	5.2	5.1	5.0	5.0

Placements

Skater A	2	2	1	1	2
Skater B	1	1	2	2	1

Skater A won the short program with a majority of firsts.
Skater B won the long program with a majority of firsts.
The short program has a factor of .5 and the long program a factor of 1.0 multiplied by placements:

	SHORT	LONG	TOTAL
RESULT			
Skater A 2nd	1 x .5 = .5	2 x 1.0 = 2.0	2.5
Skater B 1st	2 x .5 = 1.0	1 x 1.0 = 1.0	2.0

The marks that are shown on the screen are seen horizontally. You must look at the marks vertically to see where each ends up in placements and how they are factored.

Mark (Score) = Ordinal (Placement) x Factor = Result

NICE ICE

Some skaters like soft ice and others like hard ice. If the ice is too soft, a skater's blades dig in and catch. However, if the ice is too hard, the blades slip and the skater isn't secure. I like ice in the middle: hard enough so that my blades flow across it and soft enough so that my edges grip a little.

Rinks keep the surface temperature between sixteen and twenty-five degrees Fahrenheit. The ice can be hard in the middle and soft at the ends if drafts blow in the arena.

The ice surface can also be wet because a warm draft is circulating in the rink and melting the ice. Wet ice can affect your depth perception and timing in jumps when you look down to get a sense of where the ice is. If the wetness reflects what's above you, it gives you a false perception of depth. Skaters have the same problem if the ice is too white.

Painted ice and marks from skaters' blades can help your depth perception. That's why it's difficult to skate right after the Zamboni machine has smoothed the ice. A couple of scratches can help you see where the ice is.

When frost builds up on the ice, you feel like you're skating through peanut butter. You don't have any glide, so you have to work three times as hard.

Ice should be at least an inch and a half thick, especially if it's laid on top of cement. Otherwise, you can spike in your toe picks and hit the cement, which is really bad for your knees—not to mention your blades! Elvis Stojko and I both have a particular problem with thin ice because we dig in so hard with our toe picks when we jump. Sometimes we'll break a blade when it hits the cement.

When skaters go into a new rink, whether for a competition or a performance, they have to make a lot of adjustments in a short amount of time. One of the first things a skater wants to know is the size of the rink. A regulation rink is 185 by 85 feet. A European size rink is 100 by 200 feet. In big rinks, skaters set up and land jumps far from the boards. On a professional tour, skaters sometimes perform in cities with smaller rinks.

And when skaters are performing on small ice, they can even go flying into the audience!

BOO! HISS!

If people get mad about judges' decisions these days, they should keep in mind some of the scandals of the past, before television turned its unblinking eye on skating competitions. At the 1952 World Championships in Paris, for example, judges awarded France's Jacqueline du Bief the gold medal—including one perfect mark of 6.0—even though she fell twice, once skidding across the rink on her backside. The crowd booed and threw everything that could be thrown, including glass bottles, onto the ice.

Sometimes a close and unpopular decision made figure skating meets resemble hockey matches. For example, at the 1956 Olympics, the battle for gold between the Austrian and Canadian pairs was so close that accountants had to calculate the marks down to second-place ordinals to determine the winner. When it was announced that the Austrians had won, the crowd threw oranges at the judges and referees.

$\mathscr{I}$N THE PAST, SKATERS AIMED FOR THE Olympics and World Championships. Once their amateur careers were over, they turned professional. They could join traveling shows like the Ice Capades but, other than that, professional skaters didn't have a lot of choices in the type of work they could do.

Then professional competitions were created, which meant that even skaters who weren't eligible for the Olympics could challenge themselves against other great skaters.

In the last few years, there's been an explosion of interest in figure skating, which has resulted in the creation of even more professional competitions, televised specials, and skating tours.

This development has been great for the sport and for the skaters. However, the transition from amateur skating to professional skating can be one of the toughest challenges a skater will face.

(Right) After years of skating as a professional, I decided to reinstate as an amateur in 1994. Linda, as always, stands by the rail holding my shoes and skate guards, as I step on the ice to compete in my third Olympics.

In the amateur skating world, every minute of training is focused on one or two big competitions a year. The ultimate goal, of course, is winning an Olympic or World championship; that's what makes a skater's name.

A professional skater, on the other hand, spends a lot more time in the public eye than an amateur does. That means that there are a lot more times when the skater has to perform well.

Take touring, for example. The day before the tour starts, all the skaters show up with their own programs set to go. When we get together that first day, it's like old home week; everybody's saying hello and catching up. But we can't talk for long, because we have exactly one day to learn the opening and closing numbers for the show.

The next day, we hit the road. A tour may visit sixty or more cities in about three months.

If the distance between two cities requires more than four hours on the road, we fly, but otherwise we travel by bus. The bus has a small TV on it, and on long trips we watch movies on videotape. Most skaters read, sleep, listen to CDs, or talk to each other—anything to make the miles go by faster.

All that traveling inevitably results in occasional glitches. One year, my shirt for my "Music of the Night" program didn't show up until the fifth show and I had to skate in practice clothes. Another time, my costume didn't arrive and I had to borrow some clothes from Scott Davis. And in one unforgettable incident, the bag containing all my outfits fell off the bus in Minneapolis when the driver forgot to close the luggage compartment. Fortunately, some honest people found the bag by the side of the road and sent it back to me.

We sometimes have a little free time before we have to head to the arena. I usually try to find a local coffeehouse with a friend from the tour, or we'll go shopping or work out at a local health club. If we have a free evening, I might go to dinner or a movie with some of the other skaters. Most of the time, though, we're all so tired from traveling and performing that we don't have energy to go sightseeing.

Before we arrive at an arena, the crew has already set up exercise equipment, pinball machines and electronic games, a washer and dryer, and tables of food backstage. Most skaters go to the dressing room, then check the practice schedule. Depending on my practice time, I either warm up on the ice for twenty minutes or eat while I wait for my turn to skate.

The switch from amateur competition to the professional world is dramatic. Amateurs use full lighting and you can see the audience, the ice, and the boards. Professionals use theatrical lighting: darker, moodier lighting, with spotlights that follow you. It's harder to skate, because you can't see outside of that circle of light, and sometimes the lights blind you.

A good lighting director will keep half the spotlights on you and, because he knows when you're going to jump, he'll focus the other spotlights in front of you, so that you can see where you're going and what you're doing.

As a professional skater, I enjoy choreographing some of my own programs, such as this number that I skated to Frank Sinatra's version of "More."

98

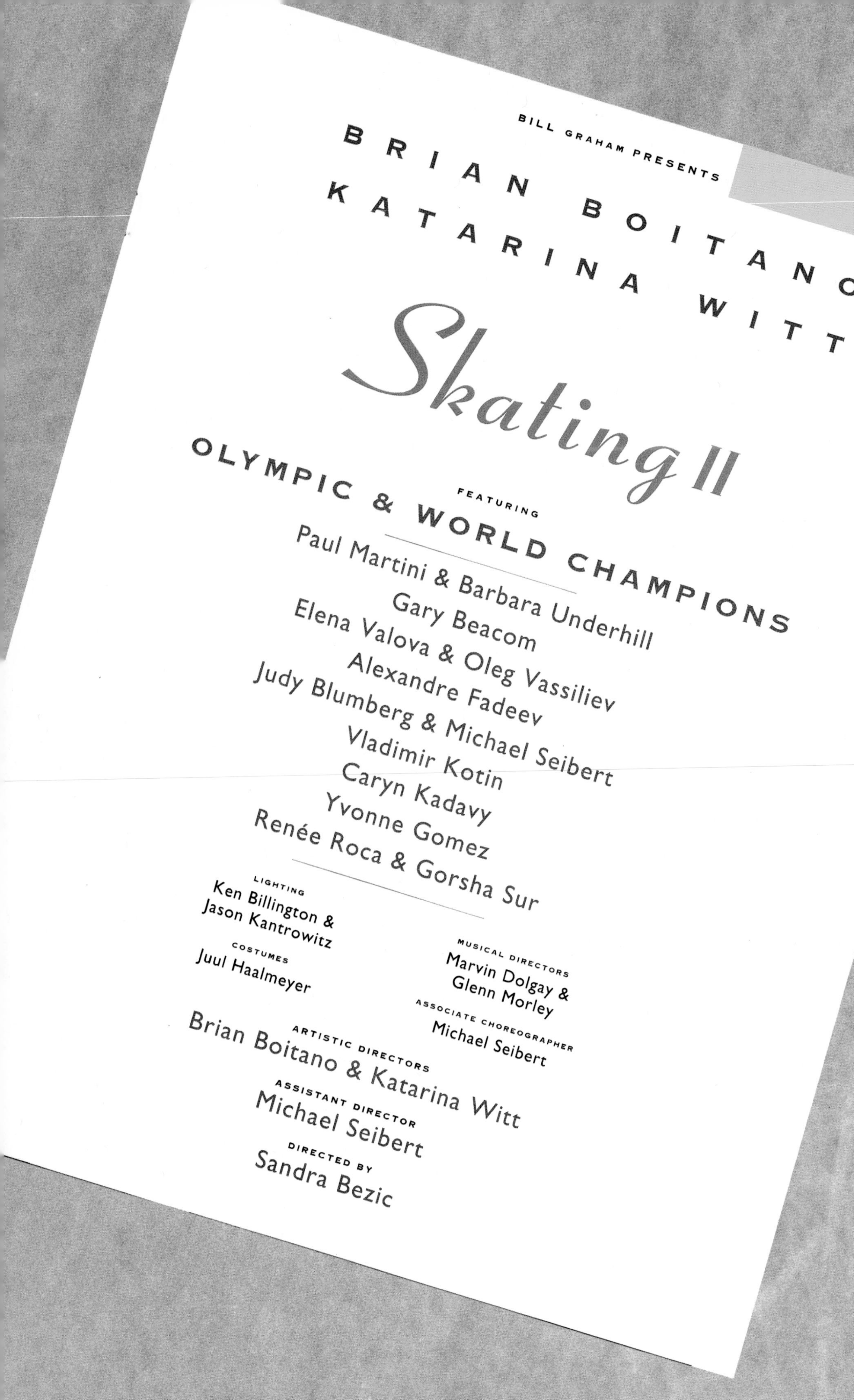

BRIAN BOITANO
KATARINA WITT

Skating II

FEATURING

OLYMPIC & WORLD CHAMPIONS

Paul Martini & Barbara Underhill
Gary Beacom
Elena Valova & Oleg Vassiliev
Alexandre Fadeev
Judy Blumberg & Michael Seibert
Vladimir Kotin
Caryn Kadavy
Yvonne Gomez
Renée Roca & Gorsha Sur

LIGHTING
Ken Billington &
Jason Kantrowitz

COSTUMES
Juul Haalmeyer

MUSICAL DIRECTORS
Marvin Dolgay &
Glenn Morley

ASSOCIATE CHOREOGRAPHER
Michael Seibert

ARTISTIC DIRECTORS
Brian Boitano & Katarina Witt

ASSISTANT DIRECTOR
Michael Seibert

DIRECTED BY
Sandra Bezic

After the 1988 Olympics, I created a series of skating tours called Skating, Skating II, and Skating 92. I asked Katarina Witt and thirteen other World and Olympic champions to skate in the shows.

I wanted to create shows that would follow a theme, rather than showcase skaters in individual, unrelated programs, and that would convey a mood of understated elegance.

The hardest part of touring is waiting backstage during the show. After a twenty-minute practice before the show and a brief skate in the opening number, skaters then must wait for the rest of the two hours for their chance to perform. We fill that dead time in various ways.

Skaters will challenge each other to pool, Ping-Pong, or pinball games; Todd Eldredge is probably the all-time pinball champ on the Campbell's Soups Tour of Champions. It's fairly useless for me to challenge the Russian skaters to a game of darts. They practice all the time, every day, so they just get one bull's-eye after another while I stand and watch.

Sometimes we'll play pranks on one another to alleviate the boredom. I admit that I once stole Oksana Baiul's costume. I returned it well before she was ready to skate—still she retaliated the next night by stealing my skates and hiding them!

On our last tour, I got hold of a squirt gun—I'll never tell how or where—and lurked around corners for days, humming the *Mission: Impossible* theme song and jumping out to squirt unsuspecting fellow skaters. They got bored with this game a long time before I did.

I've also organized contests to see who can do a sit-spin the longest without falling over (I won, but I have a feeling I'm going to be challenged to a rematch) and add-on competitions, the kind we all played when we were kids skating around the local rink. We share a great sense of camaraderie on the tour.

Skaters don't necessarily perform on every tour date.

Although touring is hard work, skaters do manage to goof around and have fun.

They may join the tour for a few weeks here or there, then leave the tour for awhile. Once I left the tour about two weeks before it ended, and all the women skaters banded together to attack the men's dressing room with whipped cream. They charged the door; each one was holding her own can of whipped cream. I tried to hold it closed, but they got in anyway. There was whipped cream everywhere, people were being thrown in the showers, everyone was laughing—that was my bon voyage party!

It's fun to be around other skaters, and I especially enjoy helping younger skaters. I talked to Michelle Kwan after she came in second at the 1997 National Championships about the pressure she felt there and the frustration of performing at less than her best. I think it helped her to talk to someone who had gone through similar experiences.

Touring is challenging for me. There's definitely a healthy competition on tour. We push each other, so we all get better and better.

But skating tours aren't the whole story. Television has brought skating to a new audience; in fact, the ratings for skating specials are so high that more and more shows are being created.

Some televised events are serious competitions for

international professional titles. Others are meant to be more fun. For example, the highest-rated skating event one year was a *Battle of the Sexes* competition. I was on the guys' team with Kurt Browning, Scott Hamilton, and Paul Wylie. We competed against the girls' team: Caryn Kadavy, Elizabeth Manley, Rosalyn Sumners, and Kristi Yamaguchi.

It was a lighthearted competition: There were celebrity judges instead of USFSA judges, and the producers asked us to put on boxing gloves and pretend to fight for the opening sequence of the show.

Then we started skating. The guys were ahead in the first half, but the girls won the spinning and jumping contest at the intermission. In the second half, the girls kept piling up the scores because the judges wanted them to catch up with the guys. Paul and I were sitting in the kiss-and-cry area saying, "We're doomed." Even if Scott got a score of 15, we knew we'd never catch up.

Then the scores came up and the announcer said, "It's a tie!" We just looked at each other in disbelief and laughed. Someone kept playing with the scores so that it would be a real nail-biter right to the end. The announcer said that each team could choose one member to participate in a jumping contest and that would determine which team won.

As soon as I heard that, I said to myself, "Uh-oh. I know what's coming."

Sure enough, my team sent me out on the ice against Kristi. She did a triple flip-double toe combination, so I had to beat that. I did a triple flip-triple toe, and the guys won, even though we were behind for most of the competition.

It's fun and relaxing to skate in those kinds of competitions. Others are just as serious and tough as amateur competitions. I still get nervous before a competition. When you're an Olympic or World champion, people expect you to skate like one. I think most of the skaters feel that way; the backstage atmosphere is just as intense as it was when we were all competing as amateurs.

The other exciting aspect about being professional involves television specials. After leaving amateur competition, I had two of the most profound experiences of my life: the filming of *Canvas of Ice* and *Carmen on Ice*.

Canvas of Ice, which aired in 1988, was the first prime-time television special by a male athlete. It represented a dream come true for me. I had always wanted to skate on

MAKEUP

Most skaters, even guys, wear makeup when they compete or perform. The main reason is that people look pale and washed out with dark circles under their eyes in bright spotlights. It's just not attractive—and part of the business is being attractive. Every skater learns to put on his or her own makeup. Even if I have a tan and I don't really need makeup, I still put it on because now it's become part of my ritual.

a glacier; the fact that I could take my skates to the middle of nowhere and do what I do best was an incredible experience for me.

It was freezing, though. I was wearing tights, a T-shirt, and a button-down shirt—that's it! It was thirty degrees below zero, so I'd skate for ten minutes, then go into a warming tent for fifteen minutes, then skate again for ten more minutes. It went on like that all day long. Sometimes an assistant would run out during a break with a thermal blanket to cover me up.

At one point, the director wanted a shot of me sliding into the snow and then just lying there. He told me to lie in the snow and that the helicopter would pull back and get a shot from the air. So I slid into the snow and waited. The helicopter didn't budge, so I kept waiting. I was getting colder and colder, but I didn't want to get up and ruin the shot, because I knew I'd have to do the whole thing over again.

Finally, the assistant ran out with the thermal blanket, yelling, "Enough, enough! He's not moving!" Maybe she thought the director had killed me. Needless to say, we didn't try for a reshoot.

Filming *Carmen on Ice* in 1989 was another wonderful experience. Katarina Witt and I had worked together before, but it was always a challenge to skate as a pair after we were both so used to competing as singles skaters.

On top of the world: Skating on an Alaskan glacier for my first TV special remains one of the highlights of my life.

Oksana Baiul

OKSANA BAIUL

I remember watching the 1988 Winter Olympics on TV when I was twelve years old and cheering for Brian. I also remember my mother watching with me and telling me to look at his wonderful arm movements. After that, I started following his career. I even put a picture of him on my wall!

Now he's become an amazing friend. For example, I was afraid to skate on tour after my car accident because I didn't know how the audience would respond. He told me, "You have to go on the ice and pretend that those twenty-five thousand people aren't just members of the audience; they're your friends." That helped a lot. And any time I'm getting ready to skate, I know he's nearby. I'll hold his hand and he'll look in my eyes and tell me not to worry. When he's not on the tour, I miss his energy.

Lloyd Eisler, Todd Eldredge, and Michelle Kwan

Todd Sand and Elvis Stojko

MICHELLE KWAN

Brian's been my idol since I was eight years old and watched him skate for the gold medal at the Olympics. Now that we're on tour together, I talk to him a lot; I ask him what it's like to be an Olympic champion. I can sense how it feels—just get a taste of it—from the way he talks about it. Every time he steps on the ice, he means business. You seldom see a skater who's finished with amateur skating and can still do all the jumps, but Brian's skating has the same quality as when he won the Olympics, maybe even better. He took skating into another dimension.

ELVIS STOJKO

I've always looked up to Brian, both because of the way he approaches his skating and the way he approaches his life. It's a very simple way of going about things: train hard, think about your skating but don't overanalyze it, and realize that everything happens for a reason.

He always pushes himself to the limit because he wants to be his best. That's hard work, but it's what has made him successful and it's been very inspiring to me.

KATARINA WITT

Katarina Witt and I have known each other for more than ten years. We first met at international competitions. After we both turned professional, we toured together in our own show. She also appeared with me in Skating Romance, Canvas of Ice, *and we starred together in* Carmen on Ice.

I first saw Brian compete in the 1986 World Championships. In 1988, we both competed at the Winter Olympics. I was good friends with Brian Orser and had hoped he would win. After I saw Brian Boitano skate, however, I thought he deserved the gold medal. I had a great deal of admiration for him, as one athlete to another, for the way he skated so well under pressure.

We really became friends after he asked me to perform in his special, *Canvas of Ice.* Then we toured together and got to know each other even better. We'd hang out with a group of skaters after the shows and either go to dinner and a movie, or have a party in one of the skaters' hotel rooms.

Sometimes we got really silly. Once Brian had a New Year's Eve party at his home in San Francisco. The new year was the Year of the Monkey, according to the Chinese calendar, so all the Russian skaters started throwing bananas out of Brian's window and into the street. It was some kind of Russian tradition—but Brian was just looking at them, like "What are they *doing?*"

When Brian and I performed together in specials, we worked long hours. One time, we were shooting a kissing scene at 5 A.M. for *Carmen on Ice,* so I ate a few chocolates to give me energy. Unfortunately, the sugar also made me giggly. Brian was on his knees and I was supposed to kiss him—but we were such good friends at that point that I would burst out in laughter every time. After the tenth try, we decided to go home and shoot the scene the next day.

We tease each other all the time—although he teases me more than I tease him!—and we always have a lot of fun. But Brian is a very good friend during tough times as well. When the Berlin Wall came down and East and West Germany were unified, the press reported that East German athletes had been given special privileges in the past and that they were now in trouble under the new political system. I think the American media exaggerated the seriousness of the situation a little and made it sound more dangerous than it was.

But Brian called me and told me that if I was in danger, I should pack my bags and go to San Francisco to stay with him. It showed me what a good friend he is—he offered me a home when he thought I needed one.

Katarina and I warm up during a long, cold night of filming Carmen on Ice *(opposite page, top), and skate together in a tour that I put together after the 1988 Olympics (opposite page, bottom). I continue to work with choreographer Sandra Bezic, who demonstrates an attitude (above) for* Carmen on Ice.

However, it was a lot of fun, and I thought Katarina's acting was brilliant. In one scene, her character was angry because I was leaving her to go to war. As I skated for her, Katarina's expression gradually changed from cold to loving; it gives me chills every time I see it. It's hard for me to watch myself, but I can watch myself in *Carmen on Ice.*

Every production like that encounters some technical problems. For example, we had ten days of solid rain. We sat on the set, hoping for the rain to stop for just five minutes so we could shoot, but it never did. That area of Spain hadn't experienced so much rain at one time in fifty years.

Plus, the ice technician had mixed dirt with the ice so

that it looked like we were skating on the ground. We had to film all our major jumping scenes right away because we completely lost the edges on our blades by the end of the shoot.

Despite the difficulties, *Carmen on Ice* is one of my proudest achievements. I'm definitely planning to do more television specials in the future.

In 1995, I formed White Canvas Productions with two partners in order to develop specials. As White Canvas's artistic director, I oversee the direction and look of the specials. Sometimes I also work as the show's director, in which case I pick the music and costumes, choreograph the opening and closing numbers, and oversee the set design, lighting, and overall flow of the show.

Although skating professionally is quite different from competing as an amateur, the number of opportunities skaters have now is amazing. There's definitely life after the Olympics.

Per Breichagen

When skaters are on tour, they sleep wherever they can, including on the tour bus. That's Michelle Kwan snoozing on my shoulder and Tara Lipinski next to her. Once the bus arrives at a rink (inset), we carry our bags into the dressing room and check out the practice schedule. We know we have a long night ahead of us.

A Tour Scrapbook

Viktor Petrenko aims for another bull's-eye (above) at one of the dart boards set up backstage. I don't even try to compete with Viktor at darts, but it's fun to practice with him (right). We'll watch each other's jumps and give advice if one of us is having a problem. Plus, we always clap for each other when one of us does a good jump.

I enjoy signing autographs after a show, although young fans are sometimes too nervous even to speak to me (left).

Oksana Baiul and I share a laugh as we're waiting to be introduced for the show's opening number (right).

Before a show starts, some skaters work out on exercise equipment that's been set up backstage (left). I watch as Dan Hollander takes on the Stairmaster and Elvis Stojko limbers up. Sometimes Tara Lipinski will ask me to watch her practice and give her advice on jumps (below).

Per Breedhagen

Part of a skater's job on tour is posing for publicity shots. Michelle Kwan, Oksana Baiul, Rudy Galindo, Nancy Kerrigan, Todd Eldredge, and I pretend to be ice fishing. Judging from our expressions, we're not having much luck!

Tonia Kwiatowski and Nicole Bobek stroke around the rink during their practice session.

Per Breedhagen

Each group of skaters— pairs, dance, men, and ladies—skate in separate practice sessions. Here Jenni Meno and Todd Sand work their program

Per Breedhagen

No one is safe backstage when I have a squirt gun in my hands!

I like inline skating in my free time because it's a good workout, but I can go much faster on ice!

I always looked up to Scott Hamilton during my amateur career. Now that we're both professionals, we have a lot of fun together; here we're posing for a publicity shot at Sun Valley.

If I had never won a single medal,
I'd still be skating in a rink
somewhere. There wouldn't be an
audience or camera flashes or autograph
seekers—but I'd still be skating.

$\mathcal{S}$KATING MOVES

When you watch skating competitions on TV, you may hear commentators talk about the skaters' "edges." Edges are the basis of skating. If you look at a skate blade, you'll see that the bottom actually curves and there is a groove in the middle of the blade. Each side of the blade is called an edge. The side that is closest to the other skate is called the inside edge; the other side is called the outside edge.

A right outside edge means that the skater is skating on the outside edge of his right foot. To be even more specific, you can say that a skater is using a right back outside edge, which means he's skating on the back outside edge of his right foot. (When he skates on both edges, it's called "skating on the flat.")

Skaters spend most of their time on one of the edges. Jumps are defined by the edge that is used for the take-off. For example, a loop jump starts on a back outside edge. The Lutz and flip jumps are the same except for the edge used for takeoff.

When judges say they're looking for "good edgework," they mean deep edges where the skater leans far over on the edge. When beginning skaters are learning their edges, they can't lean very far on the edges without falling.

The toe picks are located at the front end of the blade. They are a series of sharp spikes and are used to help the skater jump into the air on some jumps and to execute some spins.

JUMPS

Jumps are the most exciting moves in skating. Each time a skater jumps into the air, the audience holds its breath, wondering if he will land safely—or crash to the ice. The terms "single," "double," or "triple" refer to the number of times the skater rotates in the air. For example, a double toe loop means that the skater did a toe loop jump and rotated twice. A triple flip means the skater did a flip jump and rotated three times.

In 1988, Kurt Browning, Josef Sabovcik, and I started to do very difficult quadruple jumps, or quads, which require rotating four times in the air before landing. Kurt Browning landed the first quadruple jump in competition at the 1987 World Championships. Top male skaters, like Todd Eldredge, Elvis Stojko, and Michael Weiss, continue to work on perfecting their quads.

Toe loop: This jump is usually one of the first jumps that skaters learn. You take off from the back outside edge of your skating foot. Reaching back with your free foot, you plant the toe pick into the ice and vault into the air turning toward your free side. You rotate one time, then land on the same edge and same foot that you took off from. If you take off from a back inside edge and land on a back outside edge, it's called a "toe walley."

Loop: In a loop jump, the skater takes off from the back outside edge of the skating foot and lands on the same edge. It gets its name from the fact that the skates make a loop in the air. The first single loop jump was landed about 1910 by Germany's Werner Rittberger, a three-time world silver medalist. In Europe, people sometimes call this jump a "Rittberger," in his honor.

Salchow: For this jump, the skater takes off from the back inside edge of one foot and lands on the back outside edge of the other foot. It's named after Sweden's Ulrich Salchow, winner of the first Olympic Championship in 1908 and ten World Championships.

Lutz: You can usually spot a Lutz jump by the long backward glide that a skater must take before jumping. It's a hard jump because a skater approaches the jump clockwise, but then has to rotate counterclockwise in the air. (Some left-handed skaters approach counterclockwise and rotate clockwise in the air.) That means that the skater has to jump against his natural body movement. To do this jump, you take off from the back outside edge of your skating foot, using the toe pick of your free foot to vault into the air. You then land on the back outside edge of your picking foot. The jump is named for an Austrian skater named Alois Lutz, who invented it about 1913.

Flip: This jump, which is also sometimes called the "toe Salchow," is the same as the Lutz except that the skater takes off from the back inside edge instead of the back outside edge.

Axel: For most skaters, this is the hardest jump to do because you have to rotate an extra half-turn in the air. For example, a triple Axel actually requires three and a half turns in the air. It's the easiest jump to recognize when you're watching skating because it's the only jump that takes off with the skater moving forward. The skater jumps from the forward outside edge of the skating foot and lands on the back outside edge of the free foot. The jump is named for its inventor, Norway's Axel Paulsen.

SPINS

Although jumps thrill the audience, every skater must also master a number of spins. Some spins, like the death drop or the flying sit spin, also involve jumping.

Camel Spin: The skater rotates on one foot. The free leg is extended straight behind him, and the entire body is parallel to the ice.

Flying Camel Spin: The skater jumps from a forward outside edge and lands rotating in the back camel position on an outside edge.

Death Drop: The skater jumps into the air and lands in the back sit spin position.

Cross-Foot Spin: This is an upright spin in which the skater places his free foot behind his spinning foot and continues the spin on both feet with the toes together.

Layback Spin: In this upright spin, the skater drops the head and shoulders back and arches the back with the free leg extended to the side or behind. It's usually done by women skaters, although some men do perform it.

Layover Camel Spin: This is a flying camel spin in which the skater shifts his weight to spin on an outside edge, with his body turned so that he's on his side, rather than facing the ice.

Sit Spin: This spin is done in the sitting position, with the skating leg bent and the free leg extended straight in front.

I made this poster in art class when I was a freshman in high school, and gave it to my mom.

PAIR MOVES

Pair skaters must be able to perform jumps and spins separately, just as singles skaters do. However, there are many moves they do together as a team.

Death Spiral: The male skater holds his partner by one hand as he spins on one foot in a sitting position. The female skater revolves around him parallel to the ice on one foot. The move is defined by the direction the woman is moving (either forward or backward) and by the skate edge she uses.

Hand-to-hand loop lift: The man lifts his partner in front of him. They are facing the same direction as he lifts her above his head. She remains facing forward with her hands behind her.

Hydrant lift: For this lift, the man throws his partner over his head while skating backward, then rotates a half-turn and catches her as she is facing him.

Lateral twist: In this throw move, the man throws his partner overhead and she rotates in a position that's parallel to the ice before he catches her.

Platter lift: The man raises his partner overhead and holds her by her hips; her body is parallel to the ice.

Star lift: For this lift, the man raises his partner from his side, holding her hip. She is in the scissor position in the air.

Toe overhead lift: The man swings his partner from his side and behind his head. He holds her overhead as she is in the splits position; they are both facing the same direction.

Throw jumps: For these moves, the man assists, or "throws," his partner into the air and she performs the rotations of a jump and lands on one foot.

OTHER MOVES

Other moves add artistry and elegance to a skater's program.

Spiral: The skater skates either forward or backward on one foot while the free leg is raised and extended straight behind him.

Spread Eagle: The skater glides on a curve with his two heels facing each other and his toes pointing out.

The 'Tano triple Lutz

Dave Black

Scott Hamilton

SIGNATURE MOVES

Certain skaters invent new moves or do existing moves so well that they become their skating signature—the move which is closely identified with that skater.

I'm proud of having invented the 'Tano triple. Its creation was rooted in the fact that, as a youngster, I did double jumps holding one or both arms over my head.

Holding your arm over your head during a jump creates drag and makes you rotate more slowly, so you have to jump higher and with greater strength to complete your turns in the air. I figured that if my competitors did plain doubles in the short program, I would attempt something more difficult to gain an edge. That way, if everybody skated well, the judges would say, "But Boitano's double was harder."

The next step was doing the triple Lutz with my arm held over my head, the move that became known as the 'Tano triple.

Other signature moves include:

The Biellmann spin: Switzerland's Denise Biellmann starts her spin, then reaches behind her back to grasp her free foot in both hands. She gradually pulls the foot over her head, demonstrating incredible flexibility and strength.

The Hamill camel: American Dorothy Hamill created this move in which she starts out in a camel spin, then taps the blade of her free foot to the ice and lowers herself into a sit spin.

The back flip: Although many skaters perform a back flip, America's Scott Hamilton is well known for his exuberant execution of this crowd-pleasing move. France's Surya Bonaly not only does the back flip, but she lands on just one foot—the only skater in the world who can do that. Robin Cousins from Great Britain, who is almost six feet tall, is one of the few skaters to perform the back flip in a layout position.

Dave Black

The Biellmann Spin

Surya Bonaly

COMPETITION

THE RULES

For both the men's singles, ladies' singles, and pair competitions, there is a short and a long program. The short program counts for 33.3 percent of a skater's total score. During the short program, each skater must perform eight required elements: three jumps—one in a combination, three spins and two footwork sequences. The short program for pairs must include eight required elements, which include overhead lifts, side-by-side jumps, solo spins done in unison, footwork, pair spins, and a death spiral.

Judges award two marks to each skater. The first is for required elements and rates how well each element was performed. The second is for presentation and rates the overall program.

An element cannot be repeated. If, for example, a skater attempts a double Axel and falls, he can't try again. If he does, the judges must deduct a specific amount from his score.

That's why you hear commmentators say, after a skater misses a required element, "Oh, that's an automatic 0.5 deduction!"

The long program counts for 66.7 percent of a skater's total score. There are no required elements. The time limit is four minutes and thirty seconds for men and pairs, and four minutes for ladies. Again, skaters can choose their own music. The program is choreographed to showcase both artistic and technical skills.

Judges rate programs based on the difficulty of the moves, how well they're performed, and the overall presentation. Each skater is awarded two marks, the first for technical merit and the second for presentation.

Ice dancing has been an Olympic event only since 1976. This event emphasizes rhythm, musical interpretation, and precise steps; lifts and jumps aren't allowed.

The ice dancing competition is made up of three parts: two compulsory dances (which change each year and are each worth ten percent of the total score), a two-minute original dance (worth thirty percent of the total score), and a four-minute free dance (worth fifty percent of the total score).

For the two compulsory dances, each team performs the same dance—with prescribed rhythms and specific steps—to music of their choice. For the original dance, the teams skate to a prescribed rhythm, such as a rumba, again to their own music. For the free dance, skaters are allowed to select any music and choreograph the dance as inventively as they wish.

The judges' marks range from 0.0 to 6.0 based on this scale:

0 not skated
1 bad, very poor
2 poor
3 average
4 good
5 excellent
6 perfect

The marks are not added together to arrive at a skater's final score, as many people think. Instead, each judge's mark is converted into a placement. For example, if Judge A marks three skaters with 5.6, 5.8, and 5.9, the last skater is given a first-place ordinal or placement, because he received the highest score. The skater with the most number of first-place ordinals wins the event. If there's a tie, the skater with the highest presentation (artistic) mark will win the long program. The highest technical mark breaks a tie in the short program.

COMPETITION STRUCTURE

You have to belong to a USFSA-affiliated skating club or to the USFSA to enter USFSA competitions. When a skater starts out, he can compete at small competitions between skating clubs. If you win a Regional competition, you qualify to compete at a Sectional competition. The top four placers qualify for the Nationals. The medalists at the Nationals then go on to compete at the World Championships. In an Olympic year, the top winners compete at the Olympics.

(The number of skaters that each country can send to the Olympics or World Championships depends on how that country's skaters did in the previous Worlds.)

Here's how the qualifying structure for USFSA competitions leads skaters to the annual Nationals:

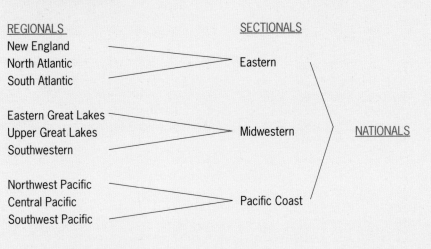

REGIONALS
New England
North Atlantic
South Atlantic

Eastern Great Lakes
Upper Great Lakes
Southwestern

Northwest Pacific
Central Pacific
Southwest Pacific

SECTIONALS
Eastern

Midwestern

Pacific Coast

NATIONALS

 FAMOUS SKATERS

Tenley Albright started skating to strengthen her back after being stricken with polio in 1946. In 1952, she won the first of five U.S. National Championships and a silver medal in the Olympics. In 1953, she became the first American woman to win the World Championships and in 1956, the first American woman to win the Olympic gold medal.

Tai Babilonia and **Randy Gardner** skated a perfect program at the 1979 World Championships to become the first U.S. pairs team in 29 years to win a world title.

Oksana Baiul combined a ballet dancer's artistry with an athlete's drive to win the 1994 Olympic ladies' gold medal at the age of sixteen, the first woman from Ukraine to do so.

Kurt Browning won the World Championships in 1989, 1990, 1991, and 1993; in 1992, he came in second. At the 1988 World Championships, this Canadian champion was the first skater to land a quadruple jump in competition (a toe loop).

Dick Button became the first American to win the Olympic gold medal in figure skating in 1948; he was also the first person to land a double Axel in competition at that Olympics. At the 1952 Olympics, he

was the first person to land a triple in competition—and won another gold medal. He won the U.S. National Championship seven times and the World Championship five times. He is the only American to ever win both the European and North American Championships.

John Curry brought an artistic quality to skating to win the first men's Olympic gold medal for his country, Great Britain, in 1976. After the Olympics, he took skating to another level by hiring choreographers to create ice ballets performed in theaters, a challenging and artistic alternative to ice shows.

Peggy Fleming won the only gold medal that the United States received in the 1968 Olympics. That was also the first Olympics that was broadcast worldwide, which turned Peggy into a worldwide celebrity.

Ekaterina Gordeeva and **Sergei Grinkov** were perhaps the ultimate pair team. The Russian husband and wife won four World Championships in 1986, 1987, 1989 and 1990, and Olympic gold medals in 1988 and 1994. They had a daughter named Daria. Sergei Grinkov died of a heart attack at a Lake Placid ice rink in 1995, at only twenty-eight years old. Ekaterina, called Katya, continues to perform as a single skater, but will

John Curry

always be remembered for her triumphs with her husband.

Gillis Grafstrom was a Swedish engineer who invented the flying sit spin and the forward inside spiral. He won three Olympic gold medals in 1920, 1924, and 1928 and one silver in 1932, plus three World titles.

Jackson Haines was born in 1840 in the United States. At that time, skaters followed the English style of skating, which was stiff, formal, and

Tenley Albright

Dick Button

The World Figure Skating Museum

The World Figure Skating Museum

Sonja Henie and Gillis Grafstrom (right)

Jackson Haines

person to skate to music and he wore fancy costumes. American critics hated his new style, so Haines went to Europe, where he put on exhibitions, became a celebrity, and invented the international style of skating we see today. He also invented the sit spin and was the first to attach his blades to his skating boots. (Before that, blades were strapped or clamped on the boots.)

Dorothy Hamill

upright, carving patterns, called "figures," on the ice. The patterns were pretty and often very elaborate, but no one would call this kind of skating exciting. Originally a dance teacher, Haines combined skating with movements from dance. He jumped into the air and did spins; he was the first

Dorothy Hamill won the Olympic gold medal in the 1976 Olympics after winning three U.S. titles. Her athleticism and joyous personality created renewed interest in ladies' figure skating.

Scott Hamilton brought real athleticism to skating and won four U.S. titles, four World titles, and the 1984 Olympic gold medal. He refused to wear costumes with spangles and beads; instead, he wore a speed skating-style outfit in competition to emphasize the athletic side of figure skating.

Carol Heiss won four straight U.S. National Championships, five consecutive World Championships and the 1960 Olympic gold medal. She married the four-time World Champion and 1956 Olympic gold medalist, Hayes Alan Jenkins.

Carol Heiss

Sonja Henie of Norway is one of the most famous women skaters in history. She entered the 1924 Olympics when she was only eleven—and performed a jump, which ladies did not do at that time. In 1927, she won the World Championships when she was fourteen; in 1928, she won the Olympic gold medal. She followed that up with two more Olympic gold medals, in 1932 and 1936, and ten World Championships. She still holds the record for the most gold medals won by any woman figure skater. She went on to become an immensely popular show skater and movie star.

Midori Ito of Japan was the first woman to land a triple Axel in a competition, at the 1989 World Championships, which she won. She brought an athleticism to figure skating that rivaled any achievements by the male figure skaters of her day.

Charlotte Oelschlagel was a show skater from Germany who went by her first name only. She became an international celebrity and, with Curt Neumann, invented the death spiral. She made the first skating film, *The Frozen Warning*, in 1917.

Axel Paulsen was a Norwegian skater who created the Axel jump in 1882. He was a speed skater as well as a figure skater; he won the first international speed-skating competition in 1885. In fact, he landed his first Axel in 1882 wearing speed skates.

The **Protopopovs, Ludmila** and **Oleg**, introduced an artistic style to the sport of pair skating. With beautiful lines, disciplined skating and a balletic approach not seen before in pair skating, the Soviet Union team won two Olympic gold medals in 1964 and 1968, before they won the first of four World Championships. They later married and moved to Switzerland to live.

Irina Rodnina skated for the Soviet Union with two different pairs partners, **Alexei Ulanov** and **Alexandr Zaitsev**. Rodnina and Ulanov won the World Championship in 1969, their first year on the international skating scene. They won the 1972 Olympic

gold medal and four World Championships. Then the pair separated and Rodnina teamed with Zaitsev. They did amazing throw lifts; Rodnina became the first woman to do a double Axel in a pairs routine. Together Rodnina and Zaitsev won six world titles and two Olympic gold medals. She is the only pair skater to ever win three Olympic gold medals.

Ulrich Salchow was a Swedish skater who invented the Salchow jump. He won ten World Championships from 1901 to 1911, nine European Championships, and the Olympic gold medal in 1908, the first year that figure skating was an Olympic event.

Madge Syers, from Great Britain, entered the World Figure Skating Championships in 1902 and shocked the skating world. The competition was open to all skaters, but no one thought women would enter. Syers placed second to Ulrich Salchow. In 1906, a separate championship was created for women. Syers won that year and again in 1907. She won the Olympic gold medal in 1908 in singles and the bronze medal in pairs with her husband Edgar. She is the only skater to ever win two medals in the same Olympics.

The World Figure Skating Museum

Sonja Henie

Ludmilla and Oleg Protopopov

Ulrich Salchow

Jayne Torvill and **Christopher Dean** reign as the world's best ice dancing team. After winning the British national title, they won four World Championships from 1981 to 1984, and the Olympic title in 1984. In winning the gold medal, they received—for the first time ever in figure skating—perfect 6.0's from all nine judges. They have toured the world with their own ice shows and continue to skate and create totally new dances.

Katarina Witt won two Olympic gold medals, the first in 1984, the second in 1988. Her "Battle of the Carmens" with American skater Debi Thomas rivaled the "Battle of the Brians" between Brian Boitano and Brian Orser in Calgary in 1988. Her technical skill, competitive spirit, and flirtatious presence on the ice created a new star.

Paul Wylie was always known in the American skating community for artistry, grace, and athleticism—but he wasn't known for winning the big competitions. At least not until the 1992 Winter Olympics in Albertville, France. He skated the performance of his life to win the silver medal. He's gone on to push the boundaries of artistry in skating as a professional.

Kristi Yamaguchi won the U.S. ladies' title in 1992, two World Championship titles in 1991 and 1992, and the Olympic gold medal in 1992. She also was the U.S. pair champion in both 1989 and 1990. She combines grace and artistry in her skating, and has gone on to a very successful professional career.

Jayne Torvill and Christopher Dean

OLYMPIC CHAMPIONS

MEN'S SINGLES

1908, London, Great Britain
Gold: Ulrich Salchow (Sweden)
Silver: Richard Johansson (Sweden)
Bronze: Per Thoren (Sweden)

1920, Antwerp, Belgium
Gold: Gillis Grafstrom (Sweden)
Silver: Andreas Krogh (Norway)
Bronze: Martin Stixrud (Norway)

1924, Chamonix, France
Gold: Gillis Grafstrom (Sweden)
Silver: Willy Boeckl (Austria)
Bronze: Georg Gautschi (Switzerland)

1928, St. Moritz, Switzerland
Gold: Gillis Grafstrom (Sweden)
Silver: Willy Boeckl (Austria)
Bronze: Robert van Zeebroeck (Belgium)

1932, Lake Placid, New York, USA
Gold: Karl Schafer (Austria)
Silver: Gillis Grafstrom (Sweden)
Bronze: Montgomery Wilson (Canada)

1936, Garmisch, Germany
Gold: Karl Schafer (Austria)
Silver: Ernst Baier (Germany)
Bronze: Felix Kaspar (Austria)

1940–1944 No Olympic Games due to World War II

1948, St. Moritz, Switzerland
Gold: Richard Button (USA)
Silver: Hans Gerschwiler (Switzerland)
Bronze: Edi Rada (Austria)

1952, Oslo, Norway
Gold: Richard Button (USA)
Silver: Helmut Seibt (Austria)
Bronze: James Grogan (USA)

1956, Cortina, Italy
Gold: Hayes A. Jenkins (USA)
Silver: Ronald Robertson (USA)
Bronze: David Jenkins (USA)

1960, Squaw Valley, California, USA
Gold: David Jenkins (USA)
Silver: Karol Divin (Czechoslovakia)
Bronze: Donald Jackson (Canada)

1964, Innsbruck, Austria
Gold: Manfred Schnelldorfer (West Germany)
Silver: Alain Calmat (France)
Bronze: Scott Allen (USA)

1968, Grenoble, France
Gold: Wolfgang Schwarz (Austria)
Silver: Tim Wood (USA)
Bronze: Patrick Pera (France)

1972, Sapporo, Japan
Gold: Ondrej Nepela (Czechoslovakia)
Silver: Sergei Chetverukhin (Soviet Union)
Bronze: Patrick Pera (France)

1976, Innsbruck, Austria
Gold: John Curry (Great Britain)
Silver: Vladimir Kovalev (Soviet Union)
Bronze: Toller Cranston (Canada)

1980, Lake Placid, New York, USA
Gold: Robin Cousins (Great Britain)
Silver: Jan Hoffmann (East Germany)
Bronze: Charles Tickner (USA)

1984, Sarajevo, Yugoslavia
Gold: Scott Hamilton (USA)
Silver: Brian Orser (Canada)
Bronze: Jozef Sabovtchik (Czechoslovakia)

1988, Calgary, Alberta, Canada
Gold: Brian Boitano (USA)
Silver: Brian Orser (Canada)
Bronze: Viktor Petrenko (Soviet Union)

1992, Albertville, France
Gold: Viktor Petrenko (Unified Team)
Silver: Paul Wylie (USA)
Bronze: Petr Barna (Czechoslovakia)

1994, Lillehammer, Norway
Gold: Alexei Urmanov (Russia)
Silver: Elvis Stojko (Canada)
Bronze: Philippe Candeloro (France)

LADIES' SINGLES

1908, London, Great Britain
Gold: Madge Syers (Great Britain)
Silver: Elsa Rendschmidt (Germany)
Bronze: Dorothy Greenhough (Great Britain)

1920, Antwerp, Belgium
Gold: Magda Julin-Mauroy (Sweden)
Silver: Svea Noren (Sweden)
Bronze: Theresa Weld (USA)

1924, Chamonix, France
Gold: Herma Plank-Szabo (Austria)
Silver: Beatrix Loughran (USA)
Bronze: Ethel Muckelt (Great Britain)

1928, St. Moritz, Switzerland
Gold: Sonja Henie (Norway)
Silver: Fritzi Burger (Austria)
Bronze: Beatrix Loughran (USA)

1932, Lake Placid, New York, USA
Gold: Sonja Henie (Norway)
Silver: Fritzi Burger (Austria)
Bronze: Maribel Vinson (USA)

1936, Garmisch, Germany
Gold: Sonja Henie (Norway)
Silver: Cecilia Colledge (Great Britain)
Bronze: Vivi-Anne Hulten (Sweden)

1940–1944 No Olympic Games due to World War II

1948, St. Moritz, Switzerland
Gold: Barbara Ann Scott (Canada)
Silver: Eva Pawlik (Austria)
Bronze: Jeannette Altwegg (Great Britain)

1952, Oslo, Norway
Gold: Jeannette Altwegg (Great Britain)
Silver: Tenley Albright (USA)
Bronze: Jacqueline du Bief (France)

1956, Cortina, Italy
Gold: Tenley Albright (USA)
Silver: Carol Heiss (USA)
Bronze: Ingrid Wendl (Austria)

1960, Squaw Valley, California, USA
Gold: Carol Heiss (USA)
Silver: Sjoukje Dijkstra (Holland)
Bronze: Barbara Roles (USA)

1964, Innsbruck, Austria
Gold: Sjoukje Dijkstra (Holland)
Silver: Regine Heitzer (Austria)
Bronze: Petra Burka (Canada)

1968, Grenoble, France
Gold: Peggy Fleming (USA)
Silver: Gabriele Seyfert (East Germany)
Bronze: Hana Maskova (Czechoslovakia)

1972, Sapporo, Japan
Gold: Beatrix Schuba (Austria)
Silver: Karen Magnussen (Canada)
Bronze: Janet Lynn (USA)

1976, Innsbruck, Austria
Gold: Dorothy Hamill (USA)
Silver: Dianne de Leeuw (Holland)
Bronze: Christine Errath (East Germany)

1980, Lake Placid, New York, USA
Gold: Anett Pötzsch (East Germany)
Silver: Linda Fratianne (USA)
Bronze: Dagmar Lurz (West Germany)

1984, Sarajevo, Yugoslavia
Gold: Katarina Witt (East Germany)
Silver: Rosalynn Sumners (USA)
Bronze: Kira Ivanova (Soviet Union)

1988, Calgary, Alberta, Canada
Gold: Katarina Witt (East Germany)
Silver: Elizabeth Manley (Canada)
Bronze: Debi Thomas (USA)

1992, Albertville, France
Gold: Kristi Yamaguchi (USA)
Silver: Midori Ito (Japan)
Bronze: Nancy Kerrigan (USA)

1994, Lillehammer, Norway
Gold: Oksana Baiul (Ukraine)
Silver: Nancy Kerrigan (USA)
Bronze: Chen Lu (China)

PAIRS

1908, London, Great Britain
Gold: Anna Hubler & Heinrich Burger (Germany)
Silver: Phyllis Johnson & James Johnson (Great Britain)
Bronze: Madge Syers & Edgar Syers (Great Britain)

1920, Antwerp, Belgium
Gold: Ludowika Jakobsson & Walter Jakobsson (Finland)
Silver: Alexia Bryn & Yngvar Bryn (Norway)
Bronze: Phyllis Johnson & Basil Williams (Great Britain)

1924, Chamonix, France
Gold: Helene Engelmann & Alfred Berger (Austria)
Silver: Ludowika Jakobsson & Walter Jakobsson (Finland)
Bronze: Andree Brunet & Pierre Brunet (France)

1928, St. Moritz, Switzerland
Gold: Andree Brunet & Pierre Brunet (France)
Silver: Lilly Scholz & Otto Kaiser (Austria)
Bronze: Melitta Brunner & Ludwig Wrede (Austria)

1932, Lake Placid, New York, USA
Gold: Andree Brunet & Pierre Brunet (France)
Silver: Beatrix Loughran & Sherwin Badger (USA)
Bronze: Emilie Rotter & Laszlo Szollas (Hungary)

1936, Garmisch, Germany
Gold: Maxi Herber & Ernst Baier (Germany)
Silver: Ilse Pausin & Erich Pausin (Austria)
Bronze: Emilie Rotter & Laszlo Szollas (Hungary)

1940–1944 No Olympic Games due to World War II

1948, St. Moritz, Switzerland
Gold: Micheline Lannoy & Pierre Baugniet (Belgium)
Silver: Andrea Kekesy & Ede Kiraly (Hungary)
Bronze: Suzanne Morrow & Wallace Distelmeyer (Canada)

1952, Oslo, Norway
Gold: Ria Falk & Paul Falk (West Germany)
Silver: Karol Kennedy & Peter Kennedy (USA)
Bronze: Marianne Nagy & Laszlo Nagy (Hungary)

1956, Cortina, Italy
Gold: Elizabeth Schwarz & Kurt Oppelt (Austria)
Silver: Frances Dafoe & Norris Bowden (Canada)
Bronze: Marianne Nagy & Laszlo Nagy (Hungary)

1960, Squaw Valley, California, USA
Gold: Barbara Wagner & Robert Paul (Canada)
Silver: Marika Kilius & Hans Baumler (West Germany)
Bronze: Nancy R. Ludington & Ronald Ludington (USA)

1964, Innsbruck, Austria
Gold: Ludmila Belousova & Oleg Protopopov (Soviet Union)
Silver: Debbi Wilkes & Guy Revell (USA)
Bronze: Vivian Joseph & Ronald Joseph (USA)

1968, Grenoble, France
Gold: Ludmila Protopopov & Oleg Protopopov (Soviet Union)
Silver: Tatiana Zhuk & Alexandr Gorelik (Soviet Union)
Bronze: Margot Glockshuber & Wolfgang Danne (West Germany)

1972, Sapporo, Japan
Gold: Irina Rodnina & Alexei Ulanov (Soviet Union)

Silver: Ludmila Smirnova & Andrei Suraikin (Soviet Union)
Bronze: Manuela Gross & Uwe Kagelmann (East Germany)

1976, Innsbruck, Austria
Gold: Irina Rodnina & Alexandr Zaitsev (Soviet Union)
Silver: Romy Kermer & Rolf Osterreich (East Germany)
Bronze: Manuela Gross & Uwe Kagelmann (East Germany)

1980, Lake Placid, New York, USA
Gold: Irina Rodnina & Alexandr Zaitsev (Soviet Union)
Silver: Marina Cherkosova & Sergei Shakrai (Soviet Union)
Bronze: Manuella Mager & Uwe Bewersdorff (East Germany)

1984, Sarajevo, Yugoslavia
Gold: Elena Valova & Oleg Vasiliev (Soviet Union)
Silver: Caitlin Carruthers & Peter Carruthers (USA)
Bronze: Larissa Selezneva & Oleg Makarov (Soviet Union)

1988, Calgary, Alberta, Canada
Gold: Ekaterina Gordeeva & Sergei Grinkov (Soviet Union)
Silver: Elena Valova & Oleg Vasiliev (Soviet Union)
Bronze: Jill Watson & Peter Oppegard (USA)

1992, Albertville, France
Gold: Natalia Mishkutenok & Artur Dmitriev (Unified Team)
Silver: Elena Bechke & Denis Petrov (Unified Team)
Bronze: Isabelle Brasseur & Lloyd Eisler (Canada)

1994, Lillehammer, Norway
Gold: Ekaterina Gordeeva & Sergei Grinkov (Russia)
Silver: Natalia Mishkutenok & Artur Dmitriev (Russia)
Bronze: Isabelle Brasseur & Lloyd Eisler (Canada)

ICE DANCING

1976, Innsbruck, Austria
Gold: Ludmila Pakhomova & Aleksandr Gorshkov (Soviet Union)
Silver: Irina Moiseeva & Andrei Minenkov (Soviet Union)
Bronze: Colleen O'Connor & Jim Millns (USA)

1980, Lake Placid, New York, USA
Gold: Natalia Linichuk & Gennadi Karponosov (Soviet Union)
Silver: Krisztina Regoczy & Andras Sallay (Hungary)
Bronze: Irina Moiseeva & Andrei Minenkov (Soviet Union)

1984, Sarajevo, Yugoslavia
Gold: Jayne Torvill & Christopher Dean (Great Britain)
Silver: Natalia Bestemianova & Andrei Bukin (Soviet Union)
Bronze: Marina Klimova & Sergei Ponomarenko (Soviet Union)

1988, Calgary, Alberta, Canada
Gold: Natalia Bestemianova & Andrei Bukin (Soviet Union)
Silver: Marina Klimova & Sergei Ponomarenko (Soviet Union)
Bronze: Tracy Wilson & Robert McCall (Canada)

1992, Albertville, France
Gold: Marina Klimova & Sergei Ponomarenko (Unified Team)
Silver: Isabelle Duchesnay & Paul Duchesnay (France)
Bronze: Maia Usova & Alexander Zhulin (Unified Team)

1994, Lillehammer, Norway
Gold: Oksana Grishuk & Evgeny Platov (Russia)
Silver: Maia Usova & Alexandr Zhulin (Russia)
Bronze: Jayne Torvill & Christopher Dean (Great Britain)

WORLD CHAMPIONSHIPS

MEN'S SINGLES

1896	Gilbert Fuchs (Germany)
1897	Gustav Hugel (Austria)
1898	Henning Grenander (Sweden)
1899	Gustav Hugel (Austria)
1900	Gustav Hugel (Austria)
1901	Ulrich Salchow (Sweden)
1902	Ulrich Salchow (Sweden)
1903	Ulrich Salchow (Sweden)
1904	Ulrich Salchow (Sweden)
1905	Ulrich Salchow (Sweden)
1906	Gilbert Fuchs (Germany)
1907	Ulrich Salchow (Sweden)
1908	Ulrich Salchow (Sweden)
1909	Ulrich Salchow (Sweden)
1910	Ulrich Salchow (Sweden)
1911	Ulrich Salchow (Sweden)
1912	Fritz Kachler (Austria)
1913	Fritz Kachler (Austria)
1914	Gosta Sandahl (Sweden)
1915–1921	no championships held due to World War I
1922	Gillis Grafstrom (Sweden)
1923	Fritz Kachler (Austria)
1924	Gillis Grafstrom (Sweden)
1925	Willy Boeckl (Austria)
1926	Willy Boeckl (Austria)
1927	Willy Boeckl (Austria)
1928	Willy Boeckl (Austria)
1929	Gillis Grafstrom (Sweden)
1930	Karl Schafer (Austria)
1931	Karl Schafer (Austria)
1932	Karl Schafer (Austria)
1933	Karl Schafer (Austria)
1934	Karl Schafer (Austria)
1935	Karl Schafer (Austria)
1936	Karl Schafer (Austria)
1937	Felix Kaspar (Austria)
1938	Felix Kaspar (Austria)
1939	Graham Sharp (Great Britain)
1940–1946	no championships held due to World War II
1947	Hans Gerschwiler (Switzerland)
1948	Richard Button (USA)
1949	Richard Button (USA)
1950	Richard Button (USA)
1951	Richard Button (USA)
1952	Richard Button (USA)
1953	Hayes Alan Jenkins (USA)
1954	Hayes Alan Jenkins (USA)
1955	Hayes Alan Jenkins (USA)
1956	Hayes Alan Jenkins (USA)
1957	David Jenkins (USA)
1958	David Jenkins (USA)
1959	David Jenkins (USA)
1960	Alain Giletti (France)
1961	no championships held due to deaths of U.S. World Team in plane crash
1962	Donald Jackson (Canada)
1963	Donald McPherson (Canada)
1964	Manfred Schnelldorfer (Canada)
1965	Alain Calmat (France)
1966	Emmerich Danzer (Austria)
1967	Emmerich Danzer (Austria)
1968	Emmerich Danzer (Austria)
1969	Tim Wood (USA)
1970	Tim Wood (USA)
1971	Ondrej Nepela (Czechoslovakia)
1972	Ondrej Nepela (Czechoslovakia)
1973	Ondrej Nepela (Czechoslovakia)
1974	Jan Hoffmann (East Germany)
1975	Sergei Volkov (Soviet Union)
1976	John Curry (Great Britain)
1977	Vladimir Kovalev (Soviet Union)
1978	Charles Tickner (USA)
1979	Vladimir Kovalev (Soviet Union)
1980	Jan Hoffmann (East Germany)
1981	Scott Hamilton (USA)
1982	Scott Hamilton (USA)
1983	Scott Hamilton (USA)
1984	Scott Hamilton (USA)
1985	Alexandr Fadeev (Soviet Union)
1986	Brian Boitano (USA)
1987	Brian Orser (Canada)
1988	Brian Boitano (USA)
1989	Kurt Browning (Canada)
1990	Kurt Browning (Canada)
1991	Kurt Browning (Canada)
1992	Viktor Petrenko (Unified Team)
1993	Kurt Browning (Canada)
1994	Elvis Stojko (Canada)
1995	Elvis Stojko (Canada)
1996	Todd Eldredge (USA)
1997	Elvis Stojko (Canada)

LADIES' SINGLES

1906	Madge Syers (Great Britain)
1907	Madge Syers (Great Britain)
1908	Lily Kronberger (Hungary)
1909	Lily Kronberger (Hungary)
1910	Lily Kronberger (Hungary)
1911	Lily Kronberger (Hungary)
1912	Opika von Horvath (Hungary)
1913	Opika von Horvath (Hungary)
1914	Opika von Horvath (Hungary)
1915–1921	no championships held due to World War I
1922	Herma Plank-Szabo (Austria)
1923	Herma Plank-Szabo (Austria)
1924	Herma Plank-Szabo (Austria)
1925	Herma Jaross-Szabo (Austria)
1926	Herma Jaross-Szabo (Austria)
1927	Sonja Henie (Norway)
1928	Sonja Henie (Norway)
1929	Sonja Henie (Norway)
1930	Sonja Henie (Norway)
1931	Sonja Henie (Norway)
1932	Sonja Henie (Norway)
1933	Sonja Henie (Norway)
1934	Sonja Henie (Norway)
1935	Sonja Henie (Norway)
1936	Sonja Henie (Norway)
1937	Cecilia Colledge (Great Britain)
1938	Megan Taylor (Great Britain)
1939	Megan Taylor (Great Britain)
1940–1946	no championships held due to World War II
1947	Barbara Ann Scott (Canada)
1948	Barbara Ann Scott (Canada)
1949	Alena Vrzanova (Czechoslovakia)
1950	Alena Vrzanova (Czechoslovakia)
1951	Jeannette Altwegg (Great Britain)
1952	Jacqueline de Bief (France)
1953	Tenley Albright (USA)
1954	Gundi Busch (West Germany)
1955	Tenley Albright (USA)
1956	Carol Heiss (USA)
1957	Carol Heiss (USA)
1958	Carol Heiss (USA)
1959	Carol Heiss (USA)
1960	Carol Heiss (USA)
1961	no championships held due to deaths of U.S. World Team in plane crash
1962	Sjoukje Dijkstra (Holland)
1963	Sjoukje Dijkstra (Holland)
1964	Sjoukje Dijkstra (Holland)
1965	Petra Burka (Canada)
1966	Peggy Fleming (USA)
1967	Peggy Fleming (USA)
1968	Peggy Fleming (USA)
1969	Gabriele Seyfert (East Germany)
1970	Gabriele Seyfert (East Germany)
1971	Beatrix Schuba (Austria)
1972	Beatrix Schuba (Austria)
1973	Karen Magnussen (Canada)
1974	Christine Errath (East Germany)
1975	Dianne de Leeuw (Holland)
1976	Dorothy Hamill (USA)
1977	Linda Fratianne (USA)
1978	Anett Pötzsch (East Germany)
1979	Linda Fratianne (USA)
1980	Anett Pötzsch (East Germany)
1981	Denise Biellmann (Switzerland)
1982	Elaine Zayak (USA)
1983	Rosalynn Sumners (USA)
1984	Katarina Witt (East Germany)
1985	Katarina Witt (East Germany)
1986	Debi Thomas (USA)
1987	Katarina Witt (East Germany)
1988	Katarina Witt (East Germany)
1989	Midori Ito (Japan)
1990	Jill Trenary (USA)
1991	Kristi Yamaguchi (USA)
1992	Kristi Yamaguchi (USA)
1993	Oksana Baiul (Ukraine)
1994	Yuka Sato (Japan)
1995	Chen Lu (China)
1996	Michelle Kwan (USA)
1997	Tara Lipinski (USA)

PAIRS

1908	Anna Hubler & Heinrich Burger (Germany)
1909	Phyllis Johnson & James Johnson (Great Britain)
1910	Anna Hubler & Heinrich Burger (Germany)
1911	Ludowika Eilers & Walter Jakobsson (Finland)
1912	Phyllis Johnson & James Johnson (Great Britain)
1913	Helene Engelmann & Karl Mejstrik (Austria)
1914	Ludowika Jakobsson & Walter Jakobsson (Finland)
1915–1921	no championships held due to World War I
1922	Helene Engelmann & Alfred Berger (Austria)
1923	Ludowika Jakobsson & Walter Jakobsson (Finland)
1924	Helene Engelmann & Alfred Berger (Austria)
1925	Herma Jaross-Szabo & Ludwig Wrede (Austria)
1926	Andree Brunet & Pierre Brunet (France)
1927	Herma Jaross-Szabo & Ludwig Wrede (Austria)
1928	Andree Brunet & Pierre Brunet (France)
1929	Lilly Scholz & Otto Kaiser (Austria)
1930	Andree Brunet & Pierre Brunet (France)
1931	Emilie Rotter & Laszlo Szollas (Hungary)
1932	Andree Brunet & Pierre Brunet (France)
1933	Emilie Rotter & Laszlo Szollas (Hungary)
1934	Emilie Rotter & Laszlo Szollas (Hungary)
1935	Emilie Rotter & Laszlo Szollas (Hungary)
1936	Maxi Herber & Ernst Baier (Germany)
1937	Maxi Herber & Ernst Baier (Germany)
1938	Maxi Herber & Ernst Baier (Germany)
1939	Maxi Herber & Ernst Baier (Germany)
1940–1946	no championships held due to World War II
1947	Micheline Lannoy & Pierre Baugniet (Belgium)
1948	Micheline Lannoy & Pierre Baugniet (Belgium)
1949	Andrea Kekesy & Ede Kiraly (Hungary)
1950	Karol Kennedy & Peter Kennedy (USA)
1951	Ria Falk & Paul Falk (West Germany)
1952	Ria Falk & Paul Falk (West Germany)
1953	Jennifer Nicks & John Nicks (Great Britain)
1954	Frances Dafoe & Norris Bowden (Canada)
1955	Frances Dafoe & Norris Bowden (Canada)
1956	Elisabeth Schwarz & Kurt Oppelt (Austria)
1957	Barbara Wagner & Robert Paul (Canada)
1958	Barbara Wagner & Robert Paul (Canada)
1959	Barbara Wagner & Robert Paul (Canada)
1960	Barbara Wagner & Robert Paul (Canada)
1961	no championships held due to deaths of U.S. World Team in plane crash
1962	Maria Jelinek & Otto Jelinek (Canada)
1963	Marika Kilius & Hans Baumler (West Germany)
1964	Marika Kilius & Hans Baumler (West Germany)
1965	Ludmila Belousova & Oleg Protopopov (Soviet Union)
1966	Ludmila Belousova & Oleg Protopopov (Soviet Union)
1967	Ludmila Belousova & Oleg Protopopov (Soviet Union)
1968	Ludmila Belousova & Oleg Protopopov (Soviet Union)
1969	Irina Rodnina & Alexei Ulanov (Soviet Union)
1970	Irina Rodnina & Alexei Ulanov (Soviet Union)
1971	Irina Rodnina & Alexei Ulanov (Soviet Union)
1972	Irina Rodnina & Alexei Ulanov (Soviet Union)
1973	Irina Rodnina & Alexandr Zaitsev (Soviet Union)
1974	Irina Rodnina & Alexandr Zaitsev (Soviet Union)
1975	Irina Rodnina & Alexandr Zaitsev (Soviet Union)
1976	Irina Rodnina & Alexandr Zaitsev (Soviet Union)
1977	Irina Rodnina & Alexandr Zaitsev (Soviet Union)
1978	Irina Rodnina & Alexandr Zaitsev (Soviet Union)
1979	Tai Babilonia & Randy Gardner (USA)
1980	Marina Cherkasova & Sergei Shakhrai (Soviet Union)
1981	Irina Vorobieva & Igor Lisovsky (Soviet Union)
1982	Sabine Baess & Tassilo Thierbach (East Germany)
1983	Elena Valova & Oleg Vasiliev (Soviet Union)
1984	Barbara Underhill & Paul Martini (Canada)
1985	Elena Valova & Oleg Vasiliev (Soviet Union)
1986	Ekaterina Gordeeva & Sergei Grinkov (Soviet Union)
1987	Ekaterina Gordeeva & Sergei Grinkov (Soviet Union)
1988	Elena Valova & Oleg Vasiliev (Soviet Union)
1989	Ekaterina Gordeeva & Sergei Grinkov (Soviet Union)
1990	Ekaterina Gordeeva & Sergei Grinkov (Soviet Union)
1991	Natalia Mishkutenok & Artur Dmitriev (Soviet Union)
1992	Natalia Mishkutenok & Artur Dmitriev (Unified Team)
1993	Isabelle Brasseur & Lloyd Eisler (Canada)
1994	Eugenia Shishkova & Vadim Naumov (Russia)
1995	Radka Kovarikova & Rene Novotny (Czechoslovakia)
1996	Evgenia Shiskova & Vadim Naumov (Russia)
1997	Mandy Woetzel & Ingo Steuer (Germany)

ICE DANCING

1952	Jean Westwood & Lawrence Demmy (Great Britain)
1953	Jean Westwood & Lawrence Demmy (Great Britain)
1954	Jean Westwood & Lawrence Demmy (Great Britain)
1955	Jean Westwood & Lawrence Demmy (Great Britain)
1956	Pamela Weight & Paul Thomas (Great Britain)
1957	June Markham & Courtney Jones (Great Britain)
1958	June Markham & Courtney Jones (Great Britain)
1959	Doreen Denny & Courtney Jones (Great Britain)
1960	Doreen Denny & Courtney Jones (Great Britain)
1961	no championships held due to deaths of U.S. World Team in plane crash
1962	Eva Romanova & Pavel Roman (Czechoslovakia)
1963	Eva Romanova & Pavel Roman (Czechoslovakia)
1964	Eva Romanova & Pavel Roman (Czechoslovakia)
1965	Eva Romanova & Pavel Roman (Czechoslovakia)
1966	Diane Towler & Bernard Ford (Great Britain)
1967	Diane Towler & Bernard Ford (Great Britain)
1968	Diane Towler & Bernard Ford (Great Britain)
1969	Diane Towler & Bernard Ford (Great Britain)
1970	Ludmila Pakhomova & Aleksandr Gorshkov (Soviet Union)
1971	Ludmila Pakhomova & Aleksandr Gorshkov (Soviet Union)
1972	Ludmila Pakhomova & Aleksandr Gorshkov (Soviet Union)
1973	Ludmila Pakhomova & Aleksandr Gorshkov (Soviet Union)
1974	Ludmila Pakhomova & Aleksandr Gorshkov (Soviet Union)
1975	Irina Moiseeva & Andrei Minenkov (Soviet Union)
1976	Ludmila Pakhomova & Aleksandr Gorshkov (Soviet Union)
1977	Irina Moiseeva & Andrei Minenkov (Soviet Union)
1978	Natalia Linichuk & Gennadi Karponosov (Soviet Union)
1979	Natalia Linichuk & Grennadi Karponosov (Soviet Union)
1980	Krisztina Regoeczy & Andras Sallay (Hungary)
1981	Jayne Torvill & Christopher Dean (Great Britain)
1982	Jayne Torvill & Christopher Dean (Great Britain)
1983	Jayne Torvill & Christopher Dean (Great Britain)
1984	Jayne Torvill & Christopher Dean (Great Britain)
1985	Natalia Bestemianova & Andrei Bukin (Soviet Union)
1986	Natalia Bestemianova & Andrei Bukin (Soviet Union)
1987	Natalia Bestemianova & Andrei Bukin (Soviet Union)
1988	Natalia Bestemianova & Andrei Bukin (Soviet Union)
1989	Marina Klimova & Sergei Ponomarenko (Soviet Union)
1990	Marina Klimova & Sergei Ponomarenko (Soviet Union)
1991	Isabelle Duchesnay & Paul Duchesnay (France)
1992	Marina Klimova & Sergei Ponomarenko (Unified Team)
1993	Maia Usova & Alexandr Zhulin (Russia)
1994	Oksana Grishuk & Evgeny Platov (Russia)
1995	Oksana Grishuk & Evgeny Platov (Russia)
1996	Oksana Grishuk & Evgeny Platov (Russia)
1997	Oksana Grishuk & Evgeny Platov (Russia)

U.S. CHAMPIONS

MEN'S SINGLES

1914	Norman M. Scott	1935	Robin Lee	1956	Hayes Alan Jenkins	1977	Charles Tickner
1915–1917	no championships held due to World War I	1936	Robin Lee	1957	David Jenkins	1978	Charles Tickner
		1937	Robin Lee	1958	David Jenkins	1979	Charles Tickner
1918	Nathaniel Niles	1938	Robin Lee	1959	David Jenkins	1980	Charles Tickner
1919	no championships held	1939	Robin Lee	1960	David Jenkins	1981	Scott Hamilton
1920	Sherwin Badger	1940	Eugene Turner	1961	Bradley Lord	1982	Scott Hamilton
1921	Sherwin Badger	1941	Eugene Turner	1962	Monty Hoyt	1983	Scott Hamilton
1922	Sherwin Badger	1942	Bobby Specht	1963	Thomas Litz	1984	Scott Hamilton
1923	Sherwin Badger	1943	Arthur Vaughn, Jr.	1964	Scott Ethan Allen	1985	Brian Boitano
1924	Sherwin Badger	1944–1945	no championships held due to World War II	1965	Gary Visconti	1986	Brian Boitano
1925	Nathaniel Niles			1966	Scott Ethan Allen	1987	Brian Boitano
1926	Chris Christenson	1946	Richard Button	1967	Gary Visconti	1988	Brian Boitano
1927	Nathaniel Niles	1947	Richard Button	1968	Tim Wood	1989	Christopher Bowman
1928	Roger Turner	1948	Richard Button	1969	Tim Wood	1990	Todd Eldredge
1929	Roger Turner	1949	Richard Button	1970	Tim Wood	1991	Todd Eldredge
1930	Roger Turner	1950	Richard Button	1971	John Misha Petkevich	1992	Christopher Bowman
1931	Roger Turner	1951	Richard Button	1972	Kenneth Shelley	1993	Scott Davis
1932	Roger Turner	1952	Richard Button	1973	Gordon McKellen, Jr.	1994	Scott Davis
1933	Roger Turner	1953	Hayes Alan Jenkins	1974	Gordon McKellen, Jr.	1995	Todd Eldredge
1934	Roger Turner	1954	Hayes Alan Jenkins	1975	Gordon McKellen, Jr.	1996	Rudy Galindo
		1955	Hayes Alan Jenkins	1976	Terry Kubicka	1997	Todd Eldredge

ICE DANCING

1936	Marjorie Parker & Joseph Savage	1951	Carmel Bodel & Edward Bodel	1966	Kristin Fortune & Dennis Sveum	1982	Judy Blumberg & Michael Seibert
1937	Nettie Prantell & Harold Hartshorne	1952	Lois Waring & Michael McGean	1967	Lorna Dyer & John Carrell	1983	Judy Blumberg & Michael Seibert
1938	Nettie Prantell & Harold Hartshorne	1953	Carol Ann Peters & Daniel Ryan	1968	Judy Schwomeyer & James Sladky	1984	Judy Blumberg & Michael Seibert
1939	Sandy MacDonald & Harold Hartshorne	1954	Carmel Bodel & Edward Bodel	1969	Judy Schwomeyer & James Sladky	1985	Judy Blumberg & Michael Seibert
1940	Sandy MacDonald & Harold Hartshorne	1955	Carmel Bodel & Edward Bodel	1970	Judy Schwomeyer & James Sladky	1986	Renee Roca & Donald Adair
1941	Sandy MacDonald & Harold Hartshorne	1956	Joan Zamboni & Roland Junso	1971	Judy Schwomeyer & James Sladky	1987	Suzanne Semanick & Scott Gregory
1942	Edith Whetstone & Alfred Richards	1957	Sharon McKenzie & Bert Wright	1972	Judy Schwomeyer & James Sladky	1988	Suzanne Semanick & Scott Gregory
1943	Marcella May & James Lochead	1958	Andree Anderson & Donald Jacoby	1973	Mary Campbell & Johnny Johns	1989	Susan Wynne & Joseph Druar
1944	Marcella May & James Lochead	1959	Andree A. Jacoby & Donald Jacoby	1974	Colleen O'Connor & Jim Millns	1990	Susan Wynne & Joseph Druar
1945	Kathe Williams & Robert Swenning	1960	Margie Ackles & Charles Phillips	1975	Colleen O'Connor & Jim Millns	1991	Elizabeth Punsalan & Jerod Swallow
1946	Anne Davies & Carleton Hoffner	1961	Dianne Sherbloom & Larry Pierce	1976	Colleen O'Connor & Jim Millns	1992	April Sargent & Russ Witherby
1947	Lois Waring & Walter Bainbridge	1962	Yvonne Littlefield & Peter Betts	1977	Judy Genovesi & Kent Weigle	1993	Renee Roca & Gorsha Sur
1948	Lois Waring & Walter Bainbridge	1963	Sally Schantz & Stanley Urban	1978	Stacey Smith & John Summers	1994	Elizabeth Punsalan & Jerod Swallow
1949	Lois Waring & Walter Bainbridge	1964	Darlene Streich & Charles Fetter	1979	Stacey Smith & John Summers	1995	Renee Roca & Gorsha Sur
1950	Lois Waring & Michael McGean	1965	Kristin Fortune & Dennis Sveum	1980	Stacey Smith & John Summers	1996	Elizabeth Punsalan & Jerod Swallow
				1981	Judy Blumberg & Michael Seibert	1997	Elizabeth Punsalan & Jerod Swallow

LADIES' SINGLES

Year	Champion	Year	Champion	Year	Champion	Year	Champion
1914	Theresa Weld	1936	Maribel Vinson	1957	Carol Heiss	1978	Linda Fratianne
1915–1917	no championships held due to World War I	1937	Maribel Vinson	1958	Carol Heiss	1979	Linda Fratianne
1918	Rosemary Beresford	1938	Joan Tozzer	1959	Carol Heiss	1980	Linda Fratianne
1919	no championships held	1939	Joan Tozzer	1960	Carol Heiss	1981	Elaine Zayak
1920	Theresa Weld	1940	Joan Tozzer	1961	Laurence Owen	1982	Rosalynn Sumners
1921	Theresa Weld Blanchard	1941	Jane Vaughn	1962	Barbara Roles	1983	Rosalynn Sumners
1922	Theresa Weld Blanchard	1942	Jane Vaughn Sullivan	1963	Lorraine Hanlon	1984	Rosalynn Sumners
1923	Theresa Weld Blanchard	1943	Gretchen Merrill	1964	Peggy Fleming	1985	Tiffany Chin
1924	Theresa Weld Blanchard	1944	Gretchen Merrill	1965	Peggy Fleming	1986	Debi Thomas
1925	Beatrix Loughran	1945	Gretchen Merrill	1966	Peggy Fleming	1987	Jill Trenary
1926	Beatrix Loughran	1946	Gretchen Merrill	1967	Peggy Fleming	1988	Debi Thomas
1927	Beatrix Loughran	1947	Gretchen Merrill	1968	Peggy Fleming	1989	Jill Trenary
1928	Maribel Vinson	1948	Gretchen Merrill	1969	Janet Lynn	1990	Jill Trenary
1929	Maribel Vinson	1949	Yvonne C. Sherman	1970	Janet Lynn	1991	Tonya Harding
1930	Maribel Vinson	1950	Yvonne C. Sherman	1971	Janet Lynn	1992	Kristi Yamaguchi
1931	Maribel Vinson	1951	Sonya Klopfer	1972	Janet Lynn	1993	Nancy Kerrigan
1932	Maribel Vinson	1952	Tenley Albright	1973	Janet Lynn	1994	vacant *
1933	Maribel Vinson	1953	Tenley Albright	1974	Dorothy Hamill	1995	Nicole Bobek
1934	Suzanne Davis	1954	Tenley Albright	1975	Dorothy Hamill	1996	Michelle Kwan
1935	Maribel Vinson	1955	Tenley Albright	1976	Dorothy Hamill	1997	Tara Lipinski
		1956	Tenley Albright	1977	Linda Fratianne		

* Tonya Harding won the 1994 U.S. Championship but was stripped of her title.

PAIRS

Year	Champions	Year	Champions	Year	Champions	Year	Champions
1914	Jeanne Chevalier & Norman M. Scott	1936	Maribel Vinson & George Hill	1958	Nancy R. Ludington & Ronald Ludington	1977	Tai Babilonia & Randy Gardner
1915–1917	no championships held due to World War I	1937	Maribel Vinson & George Hill	1959	Nancy R. Ludington & Ronald Ludington	1978	Tai Babilonia & Randy Gardner
1918	Theresa Weld & Nathaniel Niles	1938	Joan Tozzer & Bernard Fox	1960	Nancy R. Ludington & Ronald Ludington	1979	Tai Babilonia & Randy Gardner
1919	no championships held	1939	Joan Tozzer & Bernard Fox	1961	Maribel Owen & Dudley Richards	1980	Tai Babilonia & Randy Gardner
1920	Theresa Weld & Nathaniel Niles	1940	Joan Tozzer & Bernard Fox	1962	Dorothyann Nelson & Pieter Kollen	1981	Caitlin Carruthers & Peter Carruthers
1921	Theresa Weld Blanchard & Nathaniel Niles	1941	Donna Atwood & Eugene Turner	1963	Judianne Fotheringill & Jerry Fotheringill	1982	Caitlin Carruthers & Peter Carruthers
1922	Theresa Weld Blanchard & Nathaniel Niles	1942	Doris Schubach & Walter Noffke	1964	Judianne Fotheringill & Jerry Fotheringill	1983	Caitlin Carruthers & Peter Carruthers
1923	Theresa Weld Blanchard & Nathaniel Niles	1943	Doris Schubach & Walter Noffke	1965	Vivian Joseph & Ronald Joseph	1984	Caitlin Carruthers & Peter Carruthers
1924	Theresa Weld Blanchard & Nathaniel Niles	1944	Doris Schubach & Walter Noffke	1966	Cynthia Kauffman & Ronald Kauffman	1985	Jill Watson & Peter Oppegard
1925	Theresa Weld Blanchard & Nathaniel Niles	1945	Donna J. Pospisil & Jean Pierre Brunet	1967	Cynthia Kauffman & Ronald Kauffman	1986	Gillian Wachsman & Todd Waggoner
1926	Theresa Weld Blanchard & Nathaniel Niles	1946	Donna J. Pospisil & Jean Pierre Brunet	1968	Cynthia Kauffman & Ronald Kauffman	1987	Jill Watson & Peter Oppegard
1927	Theresa Weld Blanchard & Nathaniel Niles	1947	Yvonne C. Sherman & Robert Swenning	1969	Cynthia Kauffman & Ronald Kauffman	1988	Jill Watson & Peter Oppegard
1928	Maribel Vinson & Thornton Coolidge	1948	Karol Kennedy & Peter Kennedy	1970	JoJo Starbuck & Kenneth Shelley	1989	Kristi Yamaguchi & Rudy Galindo
1929	Maribel Vinson & Thornton Coolidge	1949	Karol Kennedy & Peter Kennedy	1971	JoJo Starbuck & Kenneth Shelley	1990	Kristi Yamaguchi & Rudy Galindo
1930	Beatrix Loughran & Sherwin Badger	1950	Karol Kennedy & Peter Kennedy	1972	JoJo Starbuck & Kenneth Shelley	1991	Natasha Kuchiki & Todd Sand
1931	Beatrix Loughran & Sherwin Badger	1951	Karol Kennedy & Peter Kennedy	1973	Melissa Militano & Mark Militano	1992	Calla Urbanski & Rocky Marval
1932	Beatrix Loughran & Sherwin Badger	1952	Karol Kennedy & Peter Kennedy	1974	Melissa Militano & Johnny Johns	1993	Calla Urbanski & Rocky Marval
1933	Maribel Vinson & George Hill	1953	Carole Ormaca & Robin Greiner	1975	Melissa Militano & Johnny Johns	1994	Jenni Meno & Todd Sand
1934	Grace Madden & James Lester Madden	1954	Carole Ormaca & Robin Greiner	1976	Tai Babilonia & Randy Gardner	1995	Jenni Meno & Todd Sand
1935	Maribel Vinson & George Hill	1955	Carole Ormaca & Robin Greiner			1996	Jenni Meno & Todd Sand
		1956	Carole Ormaca & Robin Greiner			1997	Kyoko Ina & Jason Dungjen
		1957	Nancy Rouillard & Ronald Ludington				

RESOURCES

ORGANIZATIONS

Canadian Figure Skating
Association (CFSA)
1600 James Naismith Drive
Suite 403
Gloucester, Ontario, K1B 5N4
Canada
(613) 748-5635
FAX: (613) 748-5718
Governing body for Canadian
figure skating, member of the
International Skating Union rep-
resenting Canada.

Ice Skating Institute of America
(ISIA)
355 West Dundee
Buffalo Grove, IL 60089
(708) 808-7528
FAX: (708) 808-8329
Offers programs for hockey,
freestyle and figures for all
ages and abilities.

International Skating Union
(ISU)
Chemin de Primerose 2
1007, Lausanne, Switzerland
(41) 21 612 66 66
FAX: (41) 21 612 66 67

Governing body for ice skating
worldwide, sets all rules governing Olympic competitions.

Professional Skaters
Association (PSA)
P.O. Box 5904
Rochester, MN 55903
(507) 281-5122
FAX: (507) 281-5491
National association for profes-
sional skaters and coaches.

U.S. Figure Skating
Association (USFSA)
20 First Street
Colorado Springs, CO 80906

(719) 635-5200
FAX: (719) 635-9548
Governing body for U.S. fig-
ure skating, member of the
International Skating Union
representing the United
States.

U.S. Olympic Committee
(USOC)
One Olympic Plaza
Colorado Springs, CO
80909
(719) 632-5551
FAX: (719) 578-4677

BOOKS

Arnold, Richard. *Dancing on Skates.* New York: St. Martin's Press, 1985.

Bailey, Donna. *Skating.* Austin, TX: Steck-Vaughn Library, 1991.

Baiul, Oksana, and Heather Alexander. *Oksana: My Own Story.* New York: Random House, 1997.

Bass, Howard. *Ice Skating.* Chicago: Rand McNally, 1980.

Berman, Alice. *Skater's Edge Sourcebook: Ice Skating Resource Guide.* Kensington, MD: Skater's Edge, 1995.

Bezic, Sandra, and David Hayes. *The Passion to Skate: An Intimate View of Figure Skating.* Atlanta: Turner Publishing, 1996.

Brennan, Christine. *Inside Edge.* New York: Scribner, 1996.

Burakoff, Alexis. *On the Ice.* Newton, MA: Hare & Hatter Books, 1994.

Button, Dick. *Dick Button on Skates.* Englewood Cliffs, N.J.: Prentice Hall, 1955.

Dolan, Edward F. *Dorothy Hamill, Olympic Skating Champion.* New York: Doubleday and Company, 1979.

Donahue, Shiobhan. *Kristi Yamaguchi, Artist on Ice.* Minneapolis: Lerner Publications Company, 1994.

Fassi, Carlo, and Gregory Smith. *Figure Skating with Carlo Fassi.* New York: Charles Scribner's Sons, 1980.

Gordeeva, Ekaterina, and E.M. Swift. *My Sergei, A Love Story.* New York: Warner Books, 1996.

Gutman, Dan. *Ice Skating: From Axels to Zambonis.* New York: Viking, 1995.

Hamill, Dorothy. *Dorothy Hamill On and Off the Ice.* New York: Alfred A. Knopf, 1983.

Hilgers, Laura. *Great Skates.* Boston: Little, Brown & Company, 1991.

Krementz, Jill. *A Very Young Skater.* New York: Alfred A. Knopf, 1979.

Ogilvie, Robert. *Competitive Figure Skating.* New York: Harper & Row, 1985.

Petkevich, John Misha. *Sports Illustrated Figure Skating: Championship Techniques.*

New York: Time Inc., 1989.

Torvill, Jayne, Christopher Dean, and Neil Wilson. *Facing the Music.* Secaucus, N.J.: Carol Publishing Group, 1995.

Trenary, Jill, and Dale Mitch. *The Day I Skated for the Gold.* New York: Simon & Schuster, 1989.

Wood, Tim. *Ice Skating.* New York: Franklin Watts, 1990.

Wright, Benjamin T. *Skating in America.* Colorado Springs, CO: U.S. Figure Skating Association, 1996.

Young, Stephanie. *Peggy Fleming: Portrait of an Ice Skater.* New York: Avon, 1984.

VIDEOS

The following companies offer video titles, many of which focus on skating.

Canadian Figure Skating
Association (CFSA)
1600 James Naismith Drive
Suite 403
Gloucester, Ontario, K1B 5N4
Canada
(613) 748-5635
FAX: (613) 748-5718

Ladin Photo & Video
22495 Madison
St. Clair Shores, MI 48081
(313) 778-8971
FAX: (313) 778-8971

Lussi Technical Video
207 Earle Avenue
Easton, MD 21601
(410) 820-6125

Professional Skaters
Association (PSA)
P.O. Box 5904
Rochester, MN 55403
(507) 281-5122
FAX: (507) 281-5491

R & J Video
P.O. Box 70287
Stockton, CA 95267
(209) 476-0124 or
(209) 466-3878

Rainbo Sports Shop
4836 North Clark Street
Chicago, IL 60640
(312) 275-5500
FAX: (312) 275-5506

The Sports Asylum, Inc.
9018 Balboa Blvd., Suite 575
Northiridge, CA 91325
(800) 929-2159
FAX: (818) 895-4763

Tohaventa Holdings, Inc.
1022 103rd Street
Edmonton, Alberta T5J 0X2,
Canada
(403) 421-8879
FAX: (403) 426-1049

U.S. Figure Skating
Association (USFSA)
20 First Street
Colorado Springs, CO
80906
(719) 635-5200
FAX: (719) 635-9548

Video Sports Productions
P.O. Box 2700
Westfield, NJ 07091
(800) USA-1996
FAX: (800) 872-1996

VIEW Video, Inc.
34 E. 23rd Street
New York, NY 10010
(800) 843-9843 or
(212) 674-5550
FAX: (212) 979-0266

MAGAZINES

Blades On Ice
Frequency: Six times a year
Published by Blades On Ice,
Inc.
7040 N. Mona Lisa Road
Tucson, AZ 85741-2633
(520) 575-1747
FAX: (520) 575-1484

International Figure Skating
Frequency: Six times a year
Published by Paragraph
Communications, Inc.
44 Front St.
Worcester, MA 01608
(508) 756-2595
FAX: (508) 792-5981

Skating
Frequency: Ten times a year
Published by the USFSA
20 First Street
Colorado Springs, CO 80906
(719) 635-5200
FAX: (719) 635-9548

American Skating World
Frequency: Twelve times a
year
Published by Group
Publications, Ltd.
1816 Brownsville Road
Pittsburgh, PA 15210
(800) 245-6280
(412) 885-7600
FAX: (412) 885-7616

PHOTO ACKNOWLEDGMENTS

The scope of this volume made it occasionally difficult, despite sincere and sustained effort, to locate photographers and/or their executors. The authors and editor regret any omissions or errors. If you wish to contact the publisher, corrections will be made in subsequent printings.

Acknowledgments

To Linda for being selfless with her time and as dedicated to detail as I am (maybe that's where I learned it); to Suzanne for listening to all I had to say and really capturing the essence; to Yvonne for being Yvonne; to Keith Sherman for being solid ground and to Anna for helping Keith stay there; to Dale Mitch, who was always a great help; to Peggy, Sandra, Oksana, Michelle (Shelly), Elvis, Kat, Joan, Bill, and Jenny Langberg, for taking time out of their busy schedules to contribute to this book; to Heinz Kluetmeier, Dino Ricci, and Lydia Stephans for supplying my memories with pictures; to Virginia and everyone at Simon & Schuster for being so passionate about this book; and to Mitchell Waters, for supporting the book from the beginning.

—Brian Boitano

I would like to thank the following people: Brian Boitano, for the inspiration of his skating and the time he devoted to creating this book; Linda Leaver, for her hard work and painstaking attention to detail; my editor, Virginia Duncan, for her energy, enthusiasm, and expert guidance; my agent, Mitchell Waters, for his tireless efforts and for championing the book from the first; associate editors Sarah Thomson and Susan Rich for their fabulous photo research; copy editor Dale Mitch for the passion he brought to both the book's text and its subject; Christy Hale for creating an elegant design; Keith Sherman and Anna Suslovsky for their help and good cheer; the staff, crew, and skaters of Campbell's Soups Tour of Champions for letting me enter their world for a while, especially Lou McClary for his backstage help; Oksana Baiul, Sandra Bezic, William Craig, Yvonne Gomez, Joan Gruber, Michelle Kwan, Elvis Stojko, and Katarina Witt for generously offering their time in interviews; and Beth Davis of the World Figure Skating Museum for technical and factual help.

—Suzanne Harper